# Life Got In The Way

Donna, wishing you
continued joy.

*[signature]*
4/20/2013

Deborah J. Davis

ISBN: 0984890459
ISBN 13: 9780984890453

# Dedication

*To my mother, Lottie Davis, who has always been there for me and always had "my back". To my father, Henry Davis, although he is no longer on this earth is always with me in spirit.*

*To my daughters, Angela Steptoe and Alexis Foster for being the phenomenal women that you are.*

*To my awesome grandchildren, Jessica, Erin, Sydney, Alex and Kalyn you make each day special for me.*

# *Acknowledgements*

Deborah Waters Lowery, thank you for encouraging me to continue writing *Life Got In The Way* when I had only completed forty-three pages. Taminka Selena Buggs, you are truly one of a kind and I am so fortunate to have you as my close friend. I cannot thank you enough for taking time from your already "way too busy" schedule to review my writings. I appreciate your invaluable support and feedback and you prodding me on when I wanted to stop. Florence Davis, not only are you an awesome sister-in-law, but I sincerely appreciate you taking time to review the initial chapters, to make sure the flow was right. Susie Green, thank you for your support and for challenging me to add the right amount of detail. Janet Foston, Novanna "Vonnie" Hunt and Shirley Patenaude, I am forever indebted to all of you for taking time and reviewing my novel with a critical eye as I approached the publishing phase.

To my creator, who gave me the inspiration to write *Life Got In The Way* and the power to make my dream a reality, I give You the highest thanks.

To my readers, thank you for reading my book!

*Deborah*

# 2007

# Chapter 1

He knew he was doing what was right, initiating things that were long overdue. These were major life changes and although he was happy, he had to acknowledge his sense of trepidation. One thing he was clear about he would not change any of his plans.

When Cameron Mitchell awoke the morning of June 30, he was pensive although he had known for months that today would be the end of his career. Twenty-seven years ago, he had started at Laney College as a part-time instructor teaching Introduction to Business Law. Later he became an adjunct professor and ultimately Dean of Instruction for the Division of Business and Math. He had actually been looking forward to today, but he had not planned on the feelings he was now having.

Cameron took his time getting out of bed and dressing for work; there was really no reason to hurry. He leisurely showered, shampooed his hair and trimmed his beard, which was definitely grayer than black these days. He maintained a trim physique. He knew he could afford to lose the ten pounds that had slowly crept on his 5'11" frame due to years of sitting behind a desk. He had packed all his clothes except a navy suit, matching shirt and tie, a pair of khakis, and a polo shirt. He completed all of his meetings earlier in the week and asked Cynthia, his secretary, not to schedule any appointments for today, so there really was no reason for professional dress.

*Today is a day of change, he thought, might as well start with a business casual look* (something he was definitely not accustomed to doing). He placed the suit in his garment bag. As he pulled on the navy polo shirt, he acknowledged that with his short salt and pepper hair, his espresso skin tone and the casual clothing, he looked damn good for 62. *I'm not usually a vain person,* he thought, as he smiled at his reflection in the mirror.

Cameron looked around the condominium to make sure that he had not left any items since he would not be returning. He leased the small, furnished unit in the Oakland Hills area when he filed for divorce from Eileen and it had served its purpose. He shipped his car and personal items last week so he left with only his travel items, and computer bag, leaving the house keys and garage genie on the kitchen counter. He placed the items in the trunk of the rental car and backed out of the garage, getting out of the vehicle and using the outside panel to close the door before leaving.

He wanted to enjoy his last day in Oakland, so he drove slowly taking the long route instead of getting on Highway 13. He drove down steep Redwood Road with its spectacular views of the Bay Area and marveled at how much the region had grown since he moved here thirty-seven years ago. There did not seem to be a vacant lot in the upscale neighborhood that abounded with expensive condominiums and houses. He decided to go down to the Flatlands, an appropriate term since there was nothing but flat land in contrast to the hill area. Today he took time to look at the sights that he had driven past for years, but never noticed because he was usually in a hurry to get to work. He looked at the shops, small businesses not yet opened, and people rushing to catch morning buses. By the time he reached International Boulevard, he could appreciate why the city renamed the busy boulevard, formerly East 14th Street, which reflected the diverse cultures that reside in the area.

He eased the rental car into his designated parking spot and forced himself to slow down from his normal quick pace as he headed to his office. He paused briefly to look around the campus. It was early, not even 7:30 a.m., yet, the campus was already bustling with students. As he climbed the steps of the Administration Building, he turned for another glimpse of the campus' neatly manicured landscape. He wanted to savor every moment of his last day. Once inside, he chose the stairs rather than the elevator, recalling the many times he had rushed up and down the stairs to a last minute meeting.

He entered his office and the truth hit him like a ton of bricks. His career was practically over. As he looked around his office, it was difficult for him to believe that he had spent much of the last twenty-seven years in various areas of the educational institution. In a few hours, it would all be history. He sat down at his desk and gazed at the bare walls, covered until a few weeks ago with awards, special mementos and commendations, and his law and education credentials. Educational books on a broad range of topics, including testing and management theories, which once lined the floor close to his desk, were packed and ready for shipment. The room seemed devoid of life, stripped of what would soon become the past.

Cameron settled back into his ergonomic chair and gazed out the window overlooking the grounds. The early morning fog was beginning to lift and the sun was timidly peering through the trees. His thoughts drifted back to when he arrived as a night school instructor on loan from his prestigious law firm. He had only planned to stay for two years. *Where had all that time gone?* His focus returned to the campus and he felt extremely proud of how Laney College had evolved.

In the early eighties, the governing board of Laney College recognized the need to be more responsive to the needs of its community. They began a series of outreach activities and program evaluations to determine the community's specific needs. Based on the results of the assessment, they implemented new courses, augmented programs and began an intense recruitment program.

The governing board changed its objective to providing greater educational opportunities for minorities, older adults, displaced homemakers, blue-collar workers, and students who performed poorly in high school. They initiated programs that would attract these individuals, while not losing focus on those students who were already attending Laney.

The board also reemphasized the benefits of two-year post-secondary education, recruited top-notch instructors who wanted to give back to the community, and implemented a hard-hitting media campaign designed to attract new students. Now Laney is renowned as one of the most innovative junior colleges in the country. A student can obtain a joint degree in a technical field, such as culinary arts or health services and simultaneously earn their Associate Degree. Matriculation increased by twenty-five percent.

Most importantly, Cameron thought, *I'm proud that I was able to play a key role in Laney's success. Now it is time to close this door; I've deviated from my own dreams for too long. So long that I've forgotten what they were. Now I need to think about what they were and if they're still important to me. It's time to get to know me again and to fulfill some dreams deferred.*

He shook his head and began removing the last contents from his desk. At the bottom lowest drawer, he came to a manila folder that contained a white envelope with aged yellowing edges. Obviously, it must have been there a long time. He didn't remember what was in it so he lifted the flap, removed the contents and his heart literally stopped for a moment. It was a picture of him and Dana taken at a quaint Italian restaurant in Montclair. The owner fawned over them and asked to take their picture; the smiling faces of a couple in love. He had seldom been that happy. Little did he know it would quickly end.

Cameron studied Dana's image in the photo her smiling round face, short curly afro haircut against reddish-brown skin, laughing eyes a deep shade of brown-black beneath thick jet-black eyelashes. He thought, *Dana was my true soul mate although I have not seen her in over twenty-five years.*

It was still painful to think of her even now. When they first met, Dana was a struggling single parent, with a young daughter and separated from her husband who had a serious drug problem. At that time, he was married and working for a prestigious law firm, but questioning his career path and his faltering marriage.

He used to keep in touch with Dana's best friend, Jackie, but it had been years since they'd spoken. Jackie was the one who told him Dana had remarried years ago and she was probably the only one who knew how deeply he was hurt by that news. He was happy for Dana; she deserved the best, but it was hard for him to accept losing her. Although they hadn't been together for years, he secretly hoped that maybe one day they would somehow reconnect. Her marriage seemed to seal that door forever.

*Now he wondered how Dana was doing.*

Cameron continued staring out the window. It was hard for him to believe that his divorce from Eileen was now final. He had been prepared to file for divorce twenty-five years ago, when he finally accepted that his marriage was over. He decided not to when Eileen was diagnosed with Multiple Sclerosis (MS).

Cameron wondered where he would be now if he had gone through with the divorce. *Would he and Dana have married? If so, what would his life with Dana have been like?*

A knock at the door interrupted Cameron's thoughts and one of his colleagues, Brad Williams, walked into his office. Cameron quickly tucked Dana's picture into his computer bag, then smiled and stood to greet Brad.

"Hey Brad, what's happening?"

"I stopped by to say good-bye, Cameron. I still cannot believe that you're leaving. Man, you're like an icon here."

Cameron laughed. "You're right, and that's exactly why it's time for me to leave."

Brad said, "I heard that you're leaving the Bay Area."

"That's true," Cameron replied. "I'll be a volunteer for the International Senior Citizens Ambassadors Organization (ISCAO); for the next two years I'll be working in impoverished areas in the United States and other parts of the world."

Brad asked, "Do you know where your first assignment will be?"

"Yes, I'll be working in Alabama, my home state."

They continued making small talk and promised to keep in touch then Brad left. Cameron finished packing and the moment finally arrived. He looked around his office one last time, and then left closing the door securely behind him.

Cynthia was sitting at her desk and she got up when he came out of the office. They briefly hugged and he told her, "You have been the best secretary I have ever had."

She smiled and said, "Thanks, you've been a great boss! You made my job easy. Now, get out of here before you miss your flight, or I start crying. Neither of which we want to happen. I have all your forwarding information and I'll handle everything."

At the door, Cameron stopped, smiled at her and said, "Check in my office, I left a little something on the desk for you."

# *Chapter 3*

It was 4 a.m. and for the last two hours, Dana Richardson had been lying awake in bed, unable to sleep. She turned on the light next to the bed, automatically dimming it as she gazed around the room. When she and Bob renovated their Cincinnati home two years ago, they made a number of changes, including removing walls in the downstairs area to give them an open floor plan. She decided that she wanted their bedroom to be a sanctuary so she used warm colors; sage green, gold and taupe, with a splash of dusty purple on the pillows and throws throughout the room. There was no television in the room. On the far wall was a waterfall that cascaded continuously. Their bedroom became a very quiet place to rest. Initially, Bob was against the "Zen type changes" as he called them, but finally agreed. Now they both appreciated the peaceful feel that exuded throughout the room.

Dana looked over at Bob, lying in the hospital bed next to her, and saw that he was resting comfortably. She got up quietly and added his bed covers; it was nice to see him sleeping peacefully, not obviously in pain. The increased pain medications, plus the hospital bed that hospice provided earlier this week, seemed to be making a difference.

She returned to bed and lay there looking around the room, thinking about how you can never imagine what life will bring you. In April, Bob began having a persistent cough that he attributed to allergies since they were having an early spring in Southern Ohio. She tried to persuade him to see his physician, since the coughing was keeping him up at night, but he kept saying he was okay. One morning in late May, he was in the bathroom getting ready for work and he began coughing up blood. By the time, he called her, he wasn't bleeding any more, but there was blood all over the bathroom floor. Dana helped him out of the bathroom, led him to a chair in their bedroom and quickly called his physician, Dr. Stoddard. She reached his answering service and left a message. He returned her call promptly and told her to bring Bob to his office right away. Dr. Stoddard saw Bob immediately when they arrived, quickly taking his vitals.

He asked Bob if he had noticed that he'd been losing weight. "My records show your weight was 185 when you had your physical two months ago, and your weight today is 173."

"I knew I had lost some weight, but I attributed it to taking your advice and cutting back on sweets."

He asked him how he had been feeling and Bob told him that he was a little tired, but nothing he was concerned about since he was working long hours on a project.

"Based on your persistent cough, you coughing up blood today, and the weight loss, I am going to order a chest x-ray so I can find out what's happening. I will have the nurse contact the x-ray department so you can get it done today. After the x-ray, I want you to go home and rest for the remainder of the day."

*I wonder why Jackie or Ashlee didn't mention it to me since we talk daily.*

Dana could not remember the last time she had read the paper or watched the news. With Bob's diagnosis of lung cancer, she decided that she could not handle the news and his illness too. Both were too depressing. As she finished reading the paper, her cell phone rang. She looked at the number. It was Jackie, who called every day. *I've been so engrossed in reading the papers that the last two hours slipped by!*

When Dana answered the phone Jackie's first question was, "Where are you?"

Dana explained that she was sitting in a coffee shop enjoying a cup of coffee and reading the paper. Then Jackie said exactly what Dana expected. "I'm glad you have a few hours to yourself."

Jackie had been pushing her to take time to get away by herself, but Dana simply could not do that. When she and Bob found out that he only had a few months to live, she told him that she would be there for him, and she would not leave him. They had plenty of friends and relatives who offered to relieve her; however, she only used them when she had to run an errand and didn't want Bob to go with her.

"I phoned the house and spoke to Bob," Jackie told her, "and he sounded good today."

As they continued talking, Dana mentioned the airline crash that she read about in the paper. "I'm so out of touch that I'd never heard about it before. Have you read that they think the pilot was drinking?"

Jackie did not respond and Dana thought that she didn't hear her.

"The plane crash where 128 people died, did you read about the findings in the paper today?"

"Yes...it was all over the news and in the papers when it happened last month." Then she quickly changed the subject and said "Ashlee and I are going to have dinner later tonight."

As Dana listened, she noticed that Jackie's voice sounded different; but when she asked her, she explained that she had been fighting a cold. Dana looked at her watch and realized that she only had fifteen minutes to get home.

"I have to go, Jackie. We'll talk tomorrow, same time."

Then she rushed out of the shop and headed to her car.

When Dana arrived home, Melissa and Maurice were coming down the stairs. They went into the kitchen and Melissa told Dana that Bob was having a relatively good day and his vitals looked fine; but unfortunately, it wouldn't be long now.

Dana closed her eyes, hugged herself, took a deep breath and regrouped. *I should know better, each time he has a good day or sleeps through the night, I think that maybe the doctors are wrong, and then...each time... I get a big dose of reality... Bob is going to die and there is absolutely nothing that I or anyone else can do at this point except make sure he's comfortable.*

After she let them out the door, Dana headed upstairs where she found Bob sitting up in bed.

"I'm glad you had some time to yourself," he said. "How was your morning?"

Dana told him about sitting at the coffee shop and reading the Enquirer. She took the small piece of bagel out of the bag and handed it to Bob who nibbled on it.

"What are you up to?"

"Nothing really, I talked to Jackie while you were out, but she didn't sound like herself."

"She called me on my cell phone and I thought she sounded different too, but she says she's fighting a cold."

Bob beckoned her to sit next to him on the hospital bed.

"Baby, how are you doing? You know we agreed that we would only do this if you could handle it. This is going to get harder. You have my permission to put me into a hospice facility at any time, or for any reason, if you can't handle this any longer."

She leaned over and kissed him on his forehead.

"That's never going to happen. I'm okay and I'm not letting you go anywhere."

Then she lay next to him until he drifted off to sleep.

1967

# Chapter 4

Cameron could not believe it was the day before his graduation from Tuskegee; the last four years had flown by. His parents would be arriving soon and he wanted to take time to do a final cleanup of his apartment before they got there. Eileen, his girlfriend, stayed over the day before and gave the place a good going over, but Cameron thought she was making sure that none of her lingerie was where his parents might find it. He surveyed his apartment and he was proud of it. He didn't have much furniture: an old sofa, a television, one chair, and a bed; everything he needed for his bachelor's pad. Album covers of some of his favorite artists were on the living room wall, including Aretha Franklin, Marvin Gaye and the Temptations. He also had an expensive stereo system that he worked hard to pay for, but it was worth it.

Eileen was anxious about meeting his parents since his dad was a Baptist minister, but he assured her that both of his parents were cool and looking forward to meeting her. He had dated regularly during his first couple of years at college, but nothing serious. He met Eileen in his senior year and initially wasn't very interested in her. She was exceptionally pretty; with her golden colored skin and petite frame, but she seemed too intense for him.

After a few dates, he discovered they had many similar goals and they had been together ever since. Lately, Eileen was spending a great deal of time at his apartment and he enjoyed her company. They had long, all night talks about what they wanted to do when they finished school. Eileen was a finance major who planned to get her Masters in Business Administration (MBA), return to her hometown and work for a bank. She felt that bank officers had a great deal of influence in small communities and could assist poor people, if they chose to. Since they were both from small towns in Alabama, they felt that their educational backgrounds would allow them to return and make a significant impact in their communities.

His dad had expected him to pursue the ministry although he had never come out directly and said so. He dropped enough unsubtle hints, such as "when you take over this ministry." Cameron never responded, but he had known for years that the church was not his calling. Last year he and his dad had gone fishing one day, and while they were out on the boat, they had a long conversation. He told his dad how much he admired him for his call to preach, but quickly added that it was not something they had in common. Cameron told his dad that he changed his major to political science with a minor in education in his sophomore year. Then he went on to tell him that he wanted to attend law school and work in the public sector. Cameron could tell that his dad was disappointed, but also very proud of him.

Over dinner this evening, he planned to tell his parents that he had received his acceptance to Boston University School of

Law and would begin in the fall. He was not going to tell them that Eileen was accepted to graduate school in the same area and that they would be living together. They were cool parents, but not that cool.

Cameron's phone rang and it was his dad calling from a nearby gas station saying that he and his mom would be there shortly. When he hung up, he glanced around the apartment and smiled. In two days, he would be out of this apartment and heading to Boston.

Thanks to his best friend, Richard Jennings, Cameron landed a position as a law clerk in a Boston firm and he would start the week following graduation. Richard worked for the firm the previous summer and they were very impressed with him. He decided not to return since he was going to pursue his MBA rather than a law degree, so he recommended Cameron for the position.

Richard had really enjoyed working in Boston last summer, so he found a job at a bank so he could return. He was one of those people who always made contacts wherever they went; he had the true gift of gab and people were drawn to him. That's why the landlord he had last summer contacted him when there was a vacancy in the building. It was a two bedroom apartment, and with Cameron working in Boston this summer, they could be roommates and split the rent. It was a great apartment with a good location on Longwood Avenue near the Boston Hospital for Women. Since they would both be working long hours, they could easily afford the rent.

Cameron had traveled a great deal with his parents, often attending church conferences, but never as far as Boston. On weekends, he and Richard explored cities throughout the northeast: Providence, Rhode Island; Portland, Maine; and

Harlem in New York. He was amazed at how a person could travel between so many states in less than an hour or two.

Eileen visited Cameron over the Fourth of July holiday; they had a great time hanging out in Boston and he even took her to New Hampshire. She was from a very poor family and had never taken a vacation, so her trip to Boston was the first time she had been out of the state of Alabama. She was a little nervous about "going to school in the North" and being away from home, but with the graduate school scholarship she received, she was not going to let her nervousness stop her.

Cameron was concerned about how he and Eileen would pay the rent in the fall since they would only be able to work part-time while attending school. Finally, he met with the landlord who assured him that he would have a one-bedroom apartment available in August; one they could easily afford.

In early August, Eileen began shipping boxes and soon the small apartment was overflowing with her belongings. She explained that in addition to saving for the rent, she had spent a considerable amount on clothing to prepare for the brutal Boston winters. She promised she would straighten it up as soon as she arrived, but it was overwhelming for Cameron.

Eileen and Cameron moved in together right before their school programs began. It was different waking up each day with her in bed beside him, far different from when they were in college with an occasional stay over. Being able to make love anytime or anywhere they wanted, without interruption, was a definite plus and their sex life went to another dimension. They both were uninhibited and enjoyed experimenting. Now they could try all of the things they had imagined when they made love. Often they would look at one another, get aroused and seize the moment. With their grueling schedules, sex was a definite outlet to alleviate stress.

One afternoon after they completed midterm exams, Eileen asked Cameron to meet her in the apartment lobby to help her with a package. After he put the package on the elevator and the door closed, Eileen leaned over, kissed him softly on his lips, then stepped back and said, "I have a surprise for you." She seductively began unbuttoning her black trench coat, revealing her nude body. Their eyes met and Cameron moved toward her, reaching to hit the elevator stop button. They immediately began kissing passionately with Cameron's strong hands moving sensuously over Eileen's body. Eileen unzipped his pants and Cameron eased her against the wall of the elevator, lifting her onto him. Soon they were both quivering as they rapidly approached orgasm. They stood against the wall, catching their breath and holding each other, until they heard someone banging for the elevator. They laughed as Eileen quickly buttoned her coat and Cameron fixed his clothes and hit the button for the elevator to resume service.

When the doors opened, several people were waiting and said they were glad to see the elevator was working because they had been waiting a while. Eileen looked at Cameron, then back at the people and said, "Yeah, we were a little worried about the elevator too, but it seems to be working fine now." Cameron winked at Eileen and she knew that they would resume as soon as they closed their apartment door. As they exited the elevator, one of their neighbors said, "Hey, you're leaving your package."

Although his relationship with Eileen was going extremely well, law school was another story. Cameron's first year in law school was the most difficult one he had ever experienced in any school. He could not believe how many times he considered dropping out, but as soon as he did, he would get a good grade on a paper that he didn't expect, and then he was right back to the grind. This was a different life, but if he could make it through his first year, he would be on the road to becoming an attorney.

With the deaths of Dr. Martin Luther King and Senator Robert Kennedy, two of the country's key advocates for social justice and equality, 1968 was a turbulent year. Cameron and Eileen routinely talked about their futures and they both acknowledged that they had concerns about returning to the South. They felt that eventually things would change in the South, but progress would be extremely slow. Both agreed that there would probably be better career opportunities in other areas of the country.

As he was approaching the end of his degree program, Cameron received a call from Richard, who had returned from a trip to the San Francisco Bay Area and was enthusiastic about the trip. He said he loved being close to the Pacific Ocean, but he was even more impressed with the lifestyle and liberal mindset.

"Man," he told Cameron, "California is a whole different world. You can be a black man out there and be successful. It's not perfect, but it's a hell of a lot better than anything in the South right now."

After that conversation, Cameron and Eileen began investigating living on the west coast and exploring job opportunities. Eileen had cousins that lived in Oakland and when she contacted them, they offered to help them if they moved to the area.

Cameron was surprised at his parents' response when he told them they were considering moving to California. "I think it's a great idea," said his dad. "I would love to have you return to Alabama, but not now. Things are still rough here and I am tired of my family members always having to struggle so hard to survive in the South. It is time for someone in my family to complete college and be able to go into their chosen field without facing so many obstacles. Go on out to the Bay Area, just make sure you have a room for your mother and I when we visit."

Cameron and Eileen were married at his father's church the summer of 1970 and moved to Oakland, California, two days after the ceremony.

*1971*

# Chapter 5

As Jackie marched into her high school gymnasium in Charlottesville, VA, she acknowledged that the decorating committee had done a miraculous job of transforming the old gym into an appropriate venue for the graduating class of 1971. There were flower arrangements on the stage, and a large banner that read "Benjamin Banneker High School Class of 1971." Although there were only 110 graduates, the room was filled to capacity. The committee had even mysteriously gotten rid of the dirty sock odor that normally permeated the room.

As she followed behind her principal and other speakers who would sit on the stage, she could see her grandmother sitting in the front row. Gran had been up late the night before making sure that everything was ready, as she said, "for today's huge event." She had baked a coconut cake, a ham, made potato salad, macaroni and cheese, and collard greens, all of Jackie's favorite foods. Not only was Jackie the first person in her family to complete high school, she was valedictorian of her class. Gran was so proud; she had a smile from ear to ear.

Gran was the only parent Jackie ever knew. Her mother, Sue, died in childbirth and her granddad died before she was born. Unfortunately, her mother never told anyone who Jackie's father was.

Over the years, Gran told Jackie stories about her mother. Sometimes they sat on the porch of their home in rural Virginia, while they were shelling beans or picking some other vegetable, and they would talk. Gran never seemed upset; she was always a direct person, so she told the stories the way she remembered them.

Gran told Jackie how happy she and her grandfather were when Sue was born. They had been married for almost two years and didn't have any children, which was unusual in those days. They were beginning to think they would never have children, when Gran discovered she was pregnant.

"Sue was beautiful, with ebony skin and dark hair, almost the color of ink. Strangers often remarked about her beauty. We spoiled her with little things we had. When we went into town, there was always someone offering to give Sue candy or some treat, even at church. Over time, Sue began to expect special treatment."

"Baby, your mama hated living in the country and having to work on the farm. Even when she was a little girl, she complained about how poor we were. She was always asking, 'Why can't we live in town?' When it was time to harvest the fields, she often wandered off. Sometimes your grandfather and I would find her daydreaming or laying down and taking a nap; doing anything except what she was supposed to do. One day, there was a sudden rainstorm while everyone was working in the fields, and when I started calling for Sue, I saw her coming toward me drenched in mud. She had been lying on a pile of dirt that quickly became mud with the sudden downpour. What a mess she was!" Gran said, laughing.

After numerous punishments, which only worked for a short time, Sue's parents told her that she didn't have to work in the fields any longer. By then they had another child; so Sue was allowed to stay home and take care of her younger sister, Mildred. This worked for a while because Sue liked watching her younger sister and didn't mind cooking, although she complained about the food.

"Your mother left home when she was sixteen and no one knew where she went. One day when we came home for supper, she was gone. She had taken all of her clothes and left. Mildred didn't have any idea where she went. We thought she might have wandered off with a drifter who'd been in the area, but there was no way to find out."

They worried, not knowing where she was. After Sue had been gone for a year, they received an envelope with no return address and a $20 bill, which they suspected was from Sue. After that, on a monthly basis, they received an envelope in the mail with a small amount of money. There was never a return address, but the postmark was always New York City.

Her father worried about her every day and even traveled to New York once to try to find her, but the city was too big. There was no way for him to locate her. He returned home depressed, never sharing with his wife what he had seen when he was in New York. One day, while he was out in the fields working, he collapsed. By the time Gran got to him, he was already gone.

Gran said, "Farm life had always been hard, but with my husband gone and a young daughter at home, it was really tough. Your granddaddy had inherited the land so after I realized that I couldn't farm all of it, I began renting acres to other farmers in the area. The farm income plus the sale of produce was enough to keep us going, but barely. When things really got rough, I would take in laundry. Those checks still arrived on a monthly basis, but suddenly they stopped."

"One day when Sue was twenty, she turned up at my door. She was obviously pregnant, but she didn't provide any details about what she had been doing, or where she had been, and why she never wrote. She cried when she found out her father died two years earlier."

"I took her in. She had changed over the years. She didn't seem to mind the farm life anymore. She helped around the house and even went out and worked the fields. I was so happy to have my oldest daughter home. It was like the Bible story where the sheep herder wasn't happy until all the sheep were in."

Many years later, Jackie overheard Gran tell one of her cousins that the day Sue died was the worst day of her life. She said she thought she only made it because when Jackie was born, she was the spitting image of her mother. Jackie and Sue looked so much alike it was eerie.

Other than being as beautiful as her mother was, Jackie was the complete opposite. Farm life did not bother her. By the time Jackie reached elementary school, her Aunt Mildred, who was like her big sister, had moved to DC.

One of her teachers noticed how intelligent she was and made sure she gave her extra work every day. Although her grandmother only had a tenth grade education, she made sure that Jackie got help with her schoolwork, when it was necessary, often from people at church.

Her aunt sent money monthly, and it was enough to support them, but they didn't have many extras. Jackie was fortunate that one of the women at the church, Miss JoAnn, who only had boys, loved to sew, so she made Jackie stylish clothes.

When Jackie entered her junior year in high school, her counselor asked her what she planned to do when she finished high school. Jackie told her she wanted to go to a local college. The counselor told Jackie that with her grade point average, she could attend almost any school in the country on full scholarship. Jackie couldn't believe it; she hadn't considered leaving Virginia. When she went home and told Gran, they were both happy, but Jackie said she wasn't sure she wanted to leave. Gran told her, "Baby, you gotta do this. I will miss you, but there's no way I will let you miss this chance."

"I won't be able to come home often. Who's going to take care of you?"

Gran answered, "The same person who's been taking care of you all these years."

Things moved extremely fast from then on; Jackie seemed to be completing college applications daily. In February, she received an acceptance with full scholarship from Wilberforce University, in Ohio. Jackie and Gran were so excited.

Now Jackie was about to deliver her high school valedictorian speech, and she thought, *thank you, Gran, for always being there for me, for being the mother, I never had.* At that moment, Jackie made a promise to herself, *I will be so successful that I will be able to take my Gran away from this hard life, and pay her back for all the sacrifices she has made for me.*

# Chapter 6

Dana could not find her cap and gown. She was sure she had put them in her closet so she went to the hallway stairs and called downstairs, "Mom, where's my cap and gown?"

"I pressed them and they're in the front hall closet."

Dana heard a car horn honk, peeked out her bedroom window and saw it was her friend, Barbara, who she was riding with to graduation.

"Wait a minute!" she yelled out the window, before she rushed down the stairs and grabbed her cap and gown out of the closet. "Bye, see you at graduation," she told her parents. Before they could respond, she was out of the house. She was so excited; graduation tonight, leaving for Rome in two days for a six-week summer enrichment program, and then off to college!

As soon as she got in the car, they both began talking at once. "Can you believe it?" Barbara asked. "In less than three hours we will be finished with high school."

She and Barbara had been good friends during most of high school. They were among the few students from their community who attended Mount Notre Dame, an all girls parochial school in Cincinnati. Dana was raised Catholic, so she always knew she would attend a Catholic high school. Barbara's mother was impressed with the school's curriculum, so she enrolled Barbara in her sophomore year.

As soon as they got to the school, they joined their classmates and prepared to get ready for the ceremony. Everyone was taking pictures and some were even crying. Their senior advisor announced that it was time to get in line. Soon the music began and the graduates entered the auditorium. Dana could see her parents and her two younger brothers, Donald and Eddie, sitting next to them.

The graduating class voted to have Rebecca Edwards, an alumnus of Mount Notre Dame, for their commencement speaker. Having a female speaker was a first for the school. Miss Edwards was a grassroots activist for women's equality and renowned internationally.

Before she began her commencement speech, she asked the graduates to stand. "You have accomplished a feat that many women in this country, and definitely in the world, are unable to achieve. I applaud you for your achievement and know that this is the beginning of a very successful life for all of you."

As she was speaking, Dana thought about how she almost blew this opportunity in her sophomore year when she got too involved with the wrong guy. He wasn't a bad person, but he was miles ahead of her and moving too fast. As a result, she got pregnant at the age of fifteen; it was the worst experience of her life. She would have done anything not to tell her parents, but she had no option. With the help of her physician and the school counselor, her parents arranged for her to go to a home for unwed mothers. The night before she was due to leave, she slipped on an icy patch and fell down their front porch steps. She blacked out and woke up in a hospital bed with her leg in a cast and her parents explained that she broke her leg when she fell. Then they broke the news to her that she had had a miscarriage.

Dana remained in the hospital for two days. She apologized to her parents repeatedly until finally her dad said, "You made a mistake, Dana, and we can't change that. Right now, we want you to put this behind you and move on."

She returned to school the following week and everyone was asking to write on the cast, clueless as to what actually had happened. She realized that not only had she hurt her parents, but also she was about to bring a life into the world, one that she was unprepared to care for. It was a revelation for her. She had seen girls in her neighborhood get pregnant at a young age and not complete high school; often ostracized by people in the community. She was fortunate to have a second chance.

As the speaker continued, Dana thought about the struggle her parents had in leaving the South to come to Ohio to make a better life for her and her brothers. She knew how hard they both worked to put them in the best schools and she knew she owed it to them to do her best.

"I challenge you, the class of 1971," the speaker was saying now, "to do as much as you can to make this world a better place, to see as much of the world as possible, and to always remember if you can dream it, you can achieve it."

Dana smiled to herself. *Yes, my dream is to see the world and in two days, I will be starting that journey!*

# Chapter 7

The summer whizzed by too fast for Jackie. She worked two jobs so she would have spending money at college, since her scholarship only included a small amount for personal items. Gran and her aunt promised to send money, but Jackie knew that they didn't have very much extra cash.

Thanks to her high school principal, she landed a job as a clerk in the legal aid office and continued working part-time at a local restaurant. Each day she assisted the attorneys by assembling case files, filing, and sometimes delivering documents to the courthouse. One of the young attorneys was impressed with how hard she worked and he took her under his wing, even allowing her to assist him in researching basic law issues. She loved sitting in the law library and poring through law books looking for a court case on point. After working there for the summer, she knew that she would definitely pursue a law degree. She wasn't sure how, but she was going to be an attorney.

It seemed like she had just graduated, but now it was time for her to leave for college. She hadn't thought that she would cry when she left for college, but last night she had cried into her pillow so Gran wouldn't hear her. She was so scared. *What if the student aide didn't meet her bus, what would she do? What if she didn't make friends?* For the last year, she had read countless teen magazines about college and dorm life, but now she thought *it's different when you're actually in the process of doing it.*

Gran and Miss JoAnn had brought her to the terminal to catch the bus early this morning. Gran was barely holding back tears as Jackie gave her one last hug before she boarded the bus. When she got to her seat, she looked out the window; Gran was still standing in the same place. She blew her a kiss as the driver put the bus in gear and she was on her way.

There weren't many people on the bus, so she had a seat to herself for the first hour. At the first stop, the bus filled up quickly and a young man boarded and sat next to her. As soon as he sat down, he began talking and told her that his name was David Mason and he was returning to college at Wilberforce University. It was his third year and he was looking forward to getting back because this year he would be a starter for the basketball team. Initially Jackie was reluctant to talk to him. After he showed her his Wilberforce ID, she loosened up and began asking all types of questions. Are college classes hard; is it easy to make friends?

David took time to answer each question and gave her advice on what courses to be careful of and which professors to avoid like the plague. He was nice and he promised to keep in touch with her when they got on campus. After all, he said he had to look out for his "home girl." Soon they both got hungry and laughed when they discovered that they had the same meal: fried chicken, potato salad and pound cake. He jokingly said this must be the "Virginia back to college by bus meal."

Jackie relaxed after talking with David and drifted off to sleep. Soon he nudged her and told her that they were in Ohio. She looked out her window and thought, *wow, I'm almost there*. Since she was fully awake now, David began giving her information about the college layout since Jackie hadn't visited the campus. He was very descriptive so she felt like she was getting a better feel for the campus, much more than she had from reading the college catalogue.

When they arrived, David helped her with her bags and introduced her to the student aide who was waiting. Then he told her he had a ride waiting and had to leave, but would see her around campus. The aide asked Jackie to stay in the area while she located the other students.

On the way to campus, it was obvious that three of the girls had attended the same high school. Jackie thought, *I never thought about getting a friend to come to college with me.*

When they arrived at Wilberforce, they were assigned to an older dorm, which reminded Jackie of a castle. It wasn't exactly what she imagined. Soon the dorm assistant arrived, introduced herself as Michelle Winters and began giving them their room assignments. Beverly, one of the girls who rode in the van to campus, got upset when she was informed she would be rooming with Jackie and not with her friend, Christine, who would be arriving later. Michelle asked for Christine's last name, checked her roster, and told her that Christine would be on another floor.

Jackie went into the room and began looking around. It wasn't exactly what she envisioned; it was old and bare, with two twin beds, two small desks and a large window that overlooked a courtyard. There was an old heater under the window and later Michelle told Jackie that she would appreciate the dorm in the winter since it was by far the warmest on campus. Jackie enjoyed decorating so she thought that the things she brought with her would brighten up the room.

Beverly came into the room and dropped her bags in the middle of the floor. Jackie asked which bed she wanted and Beverly responded, "Take any bed you want because I'm not staying here," and marched out of the room. Jackie unpacked and when she finished, she decided to go outside and find somewhere to eat. Based on her conversation with David, she was able to locate the snack shop.

When she finished eating, she walked around the campus to familiarize herself with the layout. There was a dorm meeting scheduled for later that evening, but until then she didn't have anything to do. She thought *I did not expect my first day at college to be like this.* She got a book she had brought with her, lay across her bed, and began reading.

Later that evening, she called Gran and told her about the bus ride and meeting David. She also told her about her room and that her roommate seemed okay, since she didn't want to lie. Actually, Beverly had moved out of the room and was bunking with her friends. She told Jackie, "It's not personal, they've been my friends since elementary school and I really don't want to room with a stranger."

She attended the dorm floor meeting and returned to her room when it was over and spent her first night at college alone. Although she could hear other students talking in the hallway, she decided to stay in her room. She wasn't sure exactly what she expected, but being alone in her dorm room was definitely not it. She hated to admit it, but she was a little nervous staying in the eerie castle-like building with no one in the room with her. She lay in bed scared, with the lights on, reading until she finally fell asleep.

# *Chapter 8*

For Dana summer went too fast. She felt like graduation was just a few weeks ago, but now it was time for her to head to college. Her visit to Europe surpassed her expectations. From the moment she landed in Rome, she was in love with the city, its great food, its remnants of ancient history; she was still savoring her trip. When she left, she vowed to return.

Upon returning to the States, she worked hard for the rest of the summer, so when her parents dropped her off today at the college dorm she was exhausted. Her roommate had not checked in yet and honestly, she was glad. All she wanted to do was sleep. She pulled a clean sheet out of her trunk and lay across one of the beds. When she woke up it was almost 6:00 p.m. and her roommate still hadn't arrived, so she asked Michelle about her, but she hadn't heard from her. She told her to go ahead and choose whichever bed and desk she wanted. In the meantime, the floor meeting was beginning. She was still tired after the meeting, so she headed back to her room and fell asleep fully dressed.

She felt great when she woke up! She had gotten enough rest and now she was wide-awake so she made her bed and put away her personal items. The room looked bare with only one bed made, but she figured that her roommate must have had car trouble or something.

When she finished it was 9:00 a.m. and she was due in the Financial Aid Office. The line was long when she got there so she and the student in front of her began talking. Her name was Jackie Colson and she was from Charlottesville, VA. They discovered that they were on the same floor in the dorm. By the time they reached the front of the line, they decided to have lunch together.

They went over to the campus hangout for hamburgers and fries. Jackie told her about the incident with her roommate and Dana told her that her roommate had not shown up yet. They admitted that this was not what they expected college to be like. They were surprised that so many students already knew someone. Both laughed when Dana said, "Maybe we missed the part in the college catalogue that said bring your own friend."

As they headed back to the dorm, they ran into Michelle.

"Dana," she said, "Your roommate changed her mind and won't be attending this semester."

"Can we be roommates?" Dana and Jackie asked in unison.

"No problem with me," Michelle replied, "but I'll have to check it out with the Dean of Women."

The Dean approved the room transfer and from then on, they were inseparable. They were both good students and they had their priorities straight. During the course of the year, they met and hung out with other students and went to parties, but from the beginning they became best friends, both determined to be successful.

They discussed their plans for the future and Jackie said she decided that she was tired of being poor. She had watched her Gran struggle to raise her and she was determined to be a successful attorney. Dana told her she planned to travel the world after she received her degree in social work.

When Dana found out that Jackie could not afford to go home for Thanksgiving, she invited her to come home with her. Her dad picked them up and he brought her brothers with him. Donald and Eddie were awestruck, falling in love with Jackie immediately. Dana guessed that Jackie took her looks for granted. Jackie was probably the prettiest young woman on campus, but oblivious to it. Her focus was on getting good grades and getting a full scholarship to a prestigious law school.

They had a great time during the holidays. Jackie missed her Gran since this was her first Thanksgiving away from her, but Dana's parents allowed her to call home daily and that made things easier. She enjoyed hanging out with Dana's brothers, even helping them with a science project that was due in early December. Since she did not have any siblings, Jackie thought it was fun hanging out with the boys and loved it. That weekend Jackie became part of Dana's family.

*1972*

# *Chapter* 9

Jackie was in her bedroom laying across her bed listening to music on the radio. She only had two more days before summer vacation ended and she would return to college as a sophomore.

Her first year in college was amazing, not only did she meet Dana, who quickly became her best friend, but she also excelled academically. She was on the Dean's List both semesters with a 4.0 GPA. Because of their academic records, she and Dana were among fifteen students selected to return to college two weeks early for their sophomore year to participate in a program for incoming freshmen. They would be working with the students helping them develop study skills and acting as mentors for them during their first year. Because of their involvement, they would receive a stipend for the entire year.

When Jackie returned home for the summer, she realized how much her life had changed. She had met some very nice people at college; like Dana and others who were success-oriented students.

Jackie and Dana made a promise that under no circumstance would they let their grades drop. Jackie did not want to disappoint Gran. Dana thought her parents might literally kill her if she blew her grades because she had a cousin who flunked out in her first year. Her parents were adamant that they would not have a repeat of that in their family. As a result, they did well academically and had a good time.

More importantly, Jackie finally had a best friend. Although she was involved in school and church activities when she was growing up, she never really had a best friend. When she and Dana first met, they were both apprehensive. They didn't know anyone on campus, but in the year they roomed together, they became more like sisters than roommates. They thought it was partially because neither of them had a sister. For Jackie, it was nice being able to come back to the dorm and discuss what was on her mind; talk about her goals, and not feel that there was something wrong with her wanting to be an attorney. Dana was the only person other than Gran who knew that one day she would be a very successful lawyer.

She and Dana dated a couple of guys on campus, but nothing serious. They had more fun going back to the dorm and talking about their dates than actually going out with them. In addition, David Mason, who Jackie met on the bus trip to college, took on the role of big brother and always looked out for her. It was nice having someone act as her big brother and many people thought they were actually related.

When she introduced him to Dana, he liked her immediately. He told her she could also be his little sister, "I'll make an exception for you since I don't usually deal with people from Ohio."

If he found out that either one of them had an interest in a person who was no good, he would let them know right away.

It was great having David give them the scoop on which men to avoid. A few girls had gotten involved in some ugly situations and they were glad they had avoided that path.

She remembered that Gran taught her that education is the one thing that no one can take from you. She warned her, "Be careful about getting too involved with a boy right now since you will probably not want to be with him for the rest of your life. Men are like buses, if you wait around long enough another one will always come by."

They were good at helping each other financially. Gran and Aunt Mildred sent money when they could, but a few times, she was broke. Dana received more money than she did, but occasionally she'd be broke too and waiting for her parents to send money. As a result, they formed a pact; if one had a dollar, the other could have half. Sometimes it got rough, but they always made it.

While they were packing to leave for the summer, they promised to write weekly. They knew they would room together the following year, so they planned how they would decorate their room before they left for summer break. There was no way imaginable that they would not graduate together. They had even discussed sharing an apartment during their junior year.

Now Jackie was uncertain whether she would be continuing at Wilberforce. Yesterday was her last day at Legal Aid and the director, Mr. Sherman, asked to see her after lunch. Jackie assumed he was going to tell her good-bye and let her know whether she could work at the office when she returned home for the Christmas holidays.

When she entered his office, he was sitting at his desk, and there was a large manila envelope directly in front of him. He told her to have a seat and then asked, "How did you enjoy working here this summer?"

"It was a great opportunity. I learned a great deal and I really enjoyed working with the attorneys and clients."

Then he told her that he had heard nothing but praises from the staff and even those in the courthouse research library. She looked down and thought she was in serious trouble since she was not supposed to do research. Before she could explain that she was only helping some of the attorneys who were overwhelmed with their caseload, Mr. Sherman said, "Thank you so very much. In the past, we did not allow students to do research because, in fact, we didn't think they could do it. You've been the exception to the rule; a definite asset to our team."

She sat there thinking; *at least I'm not going to be fired.*

"Are you seriously interested in becoming an attorney?"

"Well…when I started here, I didn't really know exactly what attorneys did. After seeing the difference attorneys can make in people's lives, I want to be a part of that system."

Mr. Sherman opened the envelope on his desk. "This is an application for Columbia University, one of the most prestigious Ivy League undergraduate colleges in the United States. The school also has one of the top law schools in the country."

"The attorneys here in the office have been so impressed with you that they did some research and found this full scholarship for students in their junior year of college. It does not guarantee acceptance into the law school, but every recipient who was accepted continued on to Columbia's law school on full scholarship. We feel that based on your academic performance and work at Legal Aid for the past two summers; you will be a strong contender for this scholarship. We have arranged to get you a letter of recommendation from Judge Ferguson who observed your work this summer. The attorneys in this office and I will also provide references."

"Really?"

Jackie sat there in shock, not believing what she had heard. Mr. Sherman told her that the decision would be hers and that the application needed to be submitted no later than September 30.

She thanked him, and as she was leaving his office, he handed her his business card with his direct phone number on the back, saying, "If you need any help, call me directly."

When she got home that evening, Jackie told Gran everything and they talked throughout the evening. It was such an unbelievable opportunity, but Jackie admitted she had been looking forward to graduating with her class at Wilberforce.

Gran knew how close she and Dana had become so she said, "I think you're also worried about your friendship with Dana. Soon you will find out that life is like a circle; some people come into that circle for a short time, others stay in that circle forever and distance doesn't matter. I think Dana will always be in your circle."

"If you really want to be a lawyer, fill out the papers and wait and see what happens."

She gave her a kiss and added, "You must have done a good job to get the people at Legal Aid to help you like this. I am so proud of you. I'm going to bed; this is a lot for an old person to take in one night." As she walked out of the kitchen, Jackie could hear her saying, "My granddaughter, the lawyer."

As she packed her bags, she debated whether to tell Dana she would be applying to Colombia University, or wait until she knew more.

# Chapter 10

Dana had a wonderful summer! One of the counselors from her trip to Europe heard that American Airlines was offering internships for college students and contacted her. Internships were normally for juniors, but because of her international travel experience and a good word from her counselor, they offered her a position as reservations agent. It was a great summer job, but the best thing was it would provide her a job when she came home during the holidays.

Not only was the job exactly what she wanted to do, but she met Michael Adams who worked there fulltime and attended the University of Cincinnati (UC). The first time she saw him she thought *wow, not only is he attractive, but he has an air of confidence.* Her manager assigned her to work with Michael when she completed training since they were both students. She did very well during the training course, easily mastering airline terminology, working the computer system and doing simulated bookings. She was surprised when she began answering customer calls and didn't do as well. She was clumsy when actually speaking with a passenger, getting tongue-tied and often forgetting airline codes.

After one especially difficult call, where she completely flubbed the reservation, Michael suggested that they take a walk during break. Later, they went outside and began walking around the complex, neither of them saying anything for a while.

Finally, Michael spoke, "You remind me of how nervous I was when I first began taking reservations," he said. "Like you, I did great in the classroom, but the phones were different." Then he put his hand on her right shoulder and said, "You're trying too hard, relax, making reservations is like talking to anyone else on the phone."

The feel of his hand on her shoulder seemed to penetrate through her body. They returned to work after the break and for the remainder of her shift, she did much better, but she found herself thinking about Michael. After that night, she didn't see him for a week. He was a fulltime employee with flight benefits, so he went to California for vacation. When he returned all he could talk about was moving to California and how it had always been his dream to live near the ocean.

Since they were on the same shift, they fell into the habit of having lunch together and going out after work. Many times, they would go to the park, sit, and talk. She told him a great deal about her family, how her parents, moved from Alabama when they were in their teens. That they moved to Cincinnati seeking meaningful employment away from the farmlands and the racism they experienced in the South. How both passed the Civil Service Exam and now worked for the post office.

Michael's life was definitely different from hers. He was born in a rough part of Cincinnati and both of his parents were alcoholics. His dad was a functioning alcoholic, who worked as a mechanic Monday through Friday, but was drunk all weekend. His mother was a maid in a downtown hotel. From what Michael told her, one of his parents was always drunk. They were not abusive, but definitely neglectful. Michael's older brother, Aaron, took care of him when he was young but left home as soon as he completed high school and joined the Army. Thanks to one of Michael's school counselors, he landed a full time job at American Airlines when he completed high school, which allowed him to work and attend college.

Although Michael loved the travel aspects of the job, he planned to quit as soon as he completed college. He was majoring in Hospitality Management and his dream was to manage a restaurant and ultimately open his own place. He was a fantastic cook and often brought leftovers for lunch and made sure he had enough for her. He explained that he had to learn to cook when he was a kid, or he would have starved, since he and Aaron often cooked for themselves.

One night when they were at the park, Michael told her that while he was in California, he had lined up contacts for job interviews later in the year. His plan was to leave Ohio as soon as he received his degree the next summer. He was trying to save as much money as possible, so he worked a great deal of overtime during the summer. One day, he asked her if she'd be interested in grabbing a late dinner with him when they got off work. They left work and had some burgers at a late night restaurant. All he talked about was California, all the things that he had done while he was in the San Francisco Bay Area. She heard about the cable cars, Berkeley, Oakland and the Golden Gate Bridge. He was so excited that in a year he would be living there!

She was not sure when they began dating. When they weren't at work together, they were on the phone or she was visiting him at his studio apartment; it felt natural being with him all the time. One night when they were at his apartment, he pulled out a joint and asked her if she wanted some. She was surprised. She knew people on campus who got high, but she wasn't interested.

When she told him no, he did not pressure her, but he did ask why. She explained how when she was young, she had taken a cigarette from her dad and tried to smoke it and choked so badly she thought she was going to die. She made a promise that if she didn't die and her parents didn't find out, she would never smoke. The thought of smoking made her sick. He said that was a long time ago.

You're right," she said, "but I'm still not getting high," as he continued smoking the joint.

Her parents met Michael during the summer and thought he was a nice young man. They were impressed that he was working and attending college full-time.

Dana told her parents she was due back at college two days earlier than scheduled; staying at Michael's apartment until she left for school. Although she was only nineteen, she felt grown up. She had had boyfriends in high school, but nothing serious like this.

The last morning, they were in bed and Michael pulled her into his arms and said, "Dana, I love you." She was surprised since they had not been dating very long, but she knew she cared a great deal about him.

Later, he drove her to school and she was quiet most of the way, savoring his words, "I love you." As much as she was looking forward to returning to college and seeing Jackie, she was already missing Michael. For most of the summer, they had been together almost daily. Now she would only see him on weekends when he could get off work. Since it was his last year in college, he had an extremely busy schedule. On the way to Wilberforce, he asked her if she'd be interested in moving to California.

"Maybe, when I finish college."

"I'm not talking about three years from now. I'm talking about next summer when I leave."

They had been together so much over the summer and she knew she was falling in love with him, but she did not expect this. Then he told her, "It will be easy for you to get a transfer to the west coast office of American Airlines. The college costs are low in California, so you could work and go to school like I'm doing."

I love you," he said. "I don't want to leave here without you." They had reached the campus and he pulled over and held her. Before she could say anything, he asked, "Will you think about it?"

Although she said she'd think about it, she already knew the answer. True, they had only been dating for a short time, but she simply could not envision her life without Michael.

# Chapter 11

Jackie was coming out of the dorm when Dana and Michael arrived. Dana literally jumped out of the car before Michael could park and soon both of them were hugging each other. Michael got out of the car and stood watching them. Finally, they broke their hug and Dana went back to the car, hugged Michael and said, "This is Jackie, my best friend."

Michael jokingly said, "I never would have guessed."

They all laughed and Jackie told them she was on her way to get lunch. Since Michael had time before he returned to Cincinnati, he and Dana decided to join her. They had a good time at lunch and Dana could tell that Jackie and Michael got along well. Jackie even gave Dana the thumbs up sign while Michael was paying for lunch.

They returned to the dorm, unloaded Dana's belongings, and she gave Michael a tour of the campus before he departed. With their demanding schedules, it would be at least a month before they would see each other again. Right now, a month felt like a year to her. He finally kissed her and took off down the long winding road and soon he was out of sight.

When Dana returned to their room, Jackie was down the hall talking on the phone. She couldn't wait for them to talk, but right now, she needed a little time to herself. She was amazed at how she was feeling. When Jackie returned, they both began talking at once.

Finally, Jackie said, "Okay, you go first since you have this great guy you're dating. Let's start there."

Dana told Jackie how she and Michael had met at work, and how much time they spent together during the summer. When she finished, Jackie was staring at her.

Dana asked, "What does that look mean?"

"Wow, I think you're in love. You should see that glow on your face when you say Michael's name."

"Is it that obvious?"

"Yeah, it's that obvious."

They decided to get the room organized while they were talking. Their new room was a definite improvement over their freshman dorm room. Not only was it larger but they had a private bathroom, no more sharing.

Jackie and Miss JoAnn had made some great psychedelic bedspreads. Thanks to the staff in the marketing department at American Airlines, Dana had numerous posters from around the world. Michael had also bought her posters of a few music artists, like Sly and the Family Stone, Marvin Gaye and the Jackson Five. As they put things away and hung up posters, the area materialized into a great dorm room. Neither mentioned that there might be some major changes in their lives next year.

The next morning, Jackie was leaving the Dean's office with their orientation packages when she literally ran into Gary

DuBris. He was coming in the door and she was looking down at her materials as she exited the office and didn't see him. Before they collided, he put his arm out and stopped her. When she looked up, he was smiling down at her.

"Are you okay?"

She nodded. "Yeah, sorry."

"No problem."

As she began walking away, Gary said, "Hey Jackie, what are you doing back so soon?"

She was surprised that he knew her name; there was no way he should know who she was. Gary was the school's top basketball player and this was his last year. There were rumors that he had already been offered a contract to play for a team in New York when he finished college.

"My roommate and I are back early to help with the freshman orientation."

"Great...well, I'll see you around."

Dana was impressed when Jackie got back to the room and told her about running into Gary.

"Girl, you're catching the eye of Gary DuBris – that's way up there."

Jackie said, laughing, "Yeah, like 6 foot 5 up there," and added, "he was being nice. He probably overheard the dean's secretary say my name as I left."

"Well, we'll see if he says anything else," Dana said.

That afternoon they went to the cafeteria to grab a quick lunch. They planned to review the orientation materials later in the evening after they did some last minute shopping for things for their dorm room. As soon as they sat down to eat, Dana spotted Gary entering the cafeteria. When he looked over and saw Jackie, he waved. After he went through the cafeteria line, he headed toward their table. Since Jackie's back was turned, she didn't see him approaching.

When he was next to her, he asked, "Mind if I join you?"

Before Jackie could answer, Dana said, "Sure."

He sat down and introduced himself to Dana and they all began talking as if they'd known each other forever. Gary explained that he was on campus early to help with the freshman basketball players and would be involved with the mentoring program. He told them that the coach had volunteered a few of the senior players to work with the incoming players.

"Are you going to today's orientation?"

They both looked at each other. "What orientation?"

He smiled, "You got back yesterday so you probably haven't had an opportunity to look at the materials. Orientation is in the library's large conference room at 3:00." He got up to leave, and said, "See you later."

As soon as Gary left, Dana said, "I cannot believe this, the top basketball player of the college; no, the top player in the state is interested in you."

"You're imagining things; he's not interested in me, he's a nice person."

Dana shook her head and said, "We'll see. Anyway, we need to get out of here. Obviously, we need to get back to the dorm and review our materials so we can be ready for the meeting. We can shop later."

# Chapter 12

The mentoring program was intense and Jackie and Dana were definitely earning their stipends. At the first meeting, they determined there would be five teams with three mentors on each team plus one athlete. Jackie and Dana were on the team with a student named Raymond Simpson and Gary was the athlete assigned to their team.

The teams received instructions to work closely, plan their strategy on how to handle their group, and hold weekly meetings. The mentoring program was initially for all incoming freshman; but due to costs, now it was only for students deemed to be at risk. Jackie and Gary volunteered to deliver the session on completed coursework, which was now required for all new students, resulting in them working closely together during their first two weeks on campus.

Jackie really enjoyed working with Gary. Initially she thought he was an attractive, no, very attractive man who played serious basketball. When they began working together, she discovered that he was a sensitive, intelligent person with a

3.5 GPA. They worked well together and put their own special spin on the somewhat dry material. At the end of the session, they received a round of applause. Dana told her that when she saw them together, she could see a kind of chemistry between them.

Jackie, as usual, said, "There's no chemistry, I keep telling you he's just a nice person."

She and Gary had had lunch together a couple of times when they were preparing for the presentation, but he had not said anything that indicated he was interested in her. She knew that he dated, but wasn't in a serious relationship. He tended to be somewhat of a loner and to hang out with his best friend, Jarvis Matthews and the other basketball players.

Their sophomore year flew by for Jackie and Dana. Shortly after they returned to school, they both acknowledged that they had some major decisions to make this year and they were excited for each other. Jackie had submitted her application to Columbia and was waiting for their response. She was overwhelmed with the information she received from Columbia but she and Dana reviewed it all. The pictures of the campus and dorm rooms were awesome. The thought of being able to attend college and live in New York was almost unbelievable.

Things changed as homecoming approached. Last year Dana and Jackie participated in all the homecoming activities. They went with a few girls from their dorm and had a great time. This year Dana invited Michael to come up for homecoming weekend to be her date for the dance. Jackie planned to go with some other girl friends so she was surprised when she got a call from Gary asking her to go to the dance with him. Thanks to their stipends, Jackie and Dana were not broke students this year so they were able to afford beautiful expensive dresses.

The dance was held on a warm October Indian summer evening. Jackie and Dana looked beautiful when they came down from their dorm room to meet their escorts. Jackie usually wore her hair in a ponytail, but tonight her long hair was curled and flowed against her shoulders. Dana was equally stunning with her hair in a large upswept afro making her look like an African queen.

The homecoming dance was a huge affair held in Gregory Hall and well attended since it was the biggest event of the school year. The school had outdone itself again this year by using an African theme. Colorful flags representing various African nations hung throughout the room. A local band played all the current 70's hits and the dance floor stayed full with well-dressed couples, many in African attire.

After the dance, Gary and Jackie decided to walk back to her dorm. The night was chilly so Gary put his coat around her shoulders and they held hands as they continued walking and talking.

Then Gary stopped, turned to face her directly and said earnestly, "Jackie...I'd...I'd like you to be my girlfriend."

Jackie was very touched and surprised by his proclamation, which he delivered almost as if it were a marriage proposal.

"You probably already know I really enjoy being with you. Not only are you beautiful and smart, but you're fun to be with. I feel comfortable with you. Most of the time, I feel that the girls on this campus are only interested in me as a basketball player instead of me as a person. You are the only one I've shared my dreams with; how I plan to play basketball for a few years, make some money and then go into business with my dad, who owns a mortuary.

Jackie could tell that he was nervous, so she said, "Yes, I'll be your girlfriend," adding, "I like you too."

They both smiled and then they kissed. It was a warm, sweet, undemanding kiss. They continued walking and when they reached her dorm, they kissed again before he left. Dana was still out when she got back to the room, so Jackie laid across her bed, thinking about Gary and their kiss. She could not wait to tell Dana.

During Thanksgiving break, Dana went home with Jackie since Michael had volunteered to work double shifts during the holidays. Jackie was nervous. She had stayed with Dana and her family last year during the holidays and they lived in a beautiful home in a middle class neighborhood. Jackie's home was nothing like that. It was a small three bedroom farmhouse with an indoor toilet, which she was embarrassed to admit, was added when she was thirteen.

Dana was excited; she really wanted to meet Gran. Her grandparents died when she was young but she had pleasant memories of them. She remembered the times with her grandmothers had always been special.

They laughed from the time they left campus with David who drove them to Charlottesville. Dana and David teased Jackie about not having seen how interested Gary was in her. They both told her, "You must have been blind." By now, everyone on campus knew she and Gary were dating so she took the kidding and laughed along with them.

Later Jackie questioned why she had been concerned about Dana visiting her home. They had a great time. She, Gran and Dana stayed up most of the night talking. During the visit they attended church, visited the legal aid firm, and Dana and Gran became bosom friends. By the time they left, Dana was calling her Gran and promising to write. Dana loved that she now had a 'play Gran.'

During Christmas break, Jackie received a letter from Columbia asking that she visit the college during spring break.

They would pay her airfare and that of one guest, and provide room and board. Jackie was excited and immediately asked Gran to come with her, but she declined saying, "Jackie, that would be too much for me. I know your Aunt Mildred will be away on vacation then, but I think it might be a good idea if Dana went with you."

When Jackie contacted her, Dana quickly accepted her offer and immediately began getting as much information on the city as possible. They also planned to save money so they could shop while they were there.

When Mr. Sherman, the Director at Legal Aid, told her about the potential scholarship, she was excited and nervous. She wondered if she'd be accepted, and if so, how would it be for her? She was from a small farm town would she fit in? When they began dating, she told Gary she was nervous about transferring to Columbia. They had a long discussion about what New York City was really like. Four major teams were recruiting him so he had an opportunity to visit many cities, including New York. He told her about the city's high energy level, the tall buildings, flagging down cabs, visiting Harlem, the great restaurants and going to plays. He made New York very real for her and by the time he finished she was ready to go.

In early March 1973, Jackie and Dana caught a flight to LaGuardia Airport. Bart Everson, the Columbia University representative met them at the gate with a sign that read, Jacqueline Colson. The school was located in upper Manhattan and Bart asked the driver to take a roundabout route so he could point out sights including 5th Avenue, Rockefeller Center, Park Avenue and Times Square. When they reached campus, he gave her an agenda for the week that included plenty of free time to explore the city. He even took time to explain how 5th Avenue divided the city between the east and west sides and provided them with a detailed map.

During the week, Jackie met with the dean and faculty from both the undergraduate and the law school who provided an in-depth overview of the school and its curriculum. She also met with undergrads and law school students who were scholarship recipients. All of them acknowledged that it was a rigorous program, but they had no regrets about their decision to attend Columbia. They explained that the school provided assistance, if needed, because they wanted their students to be successful.

On her final day, Jackie met with Geneva Torte, Columbia's Director of Admissions. "Well, what do you think of Columbia now that you've had a chance to look at our campus and review the curriculum?" Mrs. Torte asked.

"I love it," Jackie said, without hesitating. I'm very impressed with the physical campus, but most of all with the students who've told me it's a rigorous program, but an exciting one."

"I'm glad that you've had such a good experience during your visit, now would you like to be a part of the Columbia team?"

She was surprised; she had no idea she would receive an offer of acceptance during her visit.

"Really?"

"Yes, everyone who's met you has been impressed with you. Your academic record is outstanding, but more importantly your true passion to be an attorney is remarkable. We feel you will be an asset to the school. If you accept my offer, I will mail the official paperwork next week. Please understand that this is only an acceptance into our undergraduate program. You will need to apply to the law school, if you're still interested when you complete your undergrad studies."

"Yes. Of course, I would love to attend Columbia," Jackie said with a huge smile.

Dana had gone sightseeing while Jackie was meeting with Mrs. Torte so she wasn't in the room when Jackie returned. The school provided a phone in the room and Ms. Torte told her to feel free to make any long distance calls she wanted. First, she called Gran and told her, and she could hear Gran choke up as she said, "That's my girl, I'm so proud of you."

Next, she called Mr. Sherman and he extended his congratulations and told her he would notify everyone in the office. The next call was to Gary who was in Chicago with a basketball recruiter. She was surprised when a man answered his hotel phone. Gary had given her the number to reach him while she was gone, but she hadn't planned to call him. When he got on the line, she told him the news and she could hear noise in the background. Before she could ask what it was, Gary said, "That's Ron, another basketball player clowning around."

Then, Dana came in and Jackie told him she would talk to him when she got back to campus. When she turned around, before Dana could read the expression on her face, Jackie blurted out, "I got accepted."

They danced around the room hugging each other and then headed to Bloomingdale's to do some serious shopping, followed by dinner since they would be leaving the next day. The school provided various restaurant gift certificates and they had one left for a swank Italian restaurant. This was definitely a time to celebrate.

*1975*

# Chapter 13

Jackie got out of her seat, walked to the front of the class, handed the proctor her exam and thought, *this is it; my last exam and in two weeks, I will have my Bachelor's Degree.*

The last two years of her life at Columbia had gone by like a whirlwind. As she strode back across the campus to her dorm room, she realized that this was the first time in a long while that she didn't have anything to do. She had another week in her dorm, so there was no rush to get back and pack, and definitely no more studying.

Instead of going to her room, she headed to the park, which was located adjacent to the campus and sat on a park bench. It was a beautiful sunny day in New York, nannies were walking children and there were constant joggers running down a nearby trail. She smiled, remembering Gran asking her as she was growing up, where has the time gone? She thought it was something that old people said. Now she could identify with that feeling; the feeling that time had literally evaporated.

As she sat on the bench, she enjoyed the warm sun on her body. She reflected over the last two years and realized that everything accelerated in her life when she accepted the offer from Columbia.

Now she smiled, remembering how she and Dana had a fantastic time in New York on her visit to Columbia two years ago. Later when she returned home, Gran threw a small celebration for her. She visited the Legal Aid office where Mr. Sherman and the other attorneys in the office told her how proud they were of her. Mr. Sherman said that she was the first person he had ever known to attend such a prestigious university. He went on to say that, "You may encounter some people who feel that you were only accepted due to affirmative action laws. The only way to convince them that you're at Columbia due to merit is to continue to do the outstanding job that we've seen you do for the last two years."

When she returned from spring break that year she waited impatiently for Dana to arrive since she had called and told her she had a surprise for her. When Dana finally burst through the dorm room door, she had a wide smile on her face.

"Can't you see?"

Jackie was looking at her, but she didn't see anything noticeably different until Dana lifted her left hand.

"Is that what I think it is?"

"Yes, it's an engagement ring. Michael and I are getting married this summer before we leave for California."

Jackie was shocked; they had both discussed getting married, but only as something in the future, not now. Before she could say anything, Dana told her how Michael had proposed and she accepted. Since Dana knew her parents would not be pleased, she and Michael had wrote a plan of exactly what to tell them.

They met with her parents and, as expected, both objected to the idea of Dana getting married, citing the fact that they had not known each other that long. Dana and Michael had an answer for each of their concerns. First, Dana pointed out that her godparents had married after knowing each other only three months and even her parents talked about what a great relationship they had.

"What about finishing college?" her mother asked.

"I'm applying now; I'll finish any requirements at the junior college and transfer to a four year college."

"What about housing?"

"Michael found an apartment on his last trip."

"What about jobs?"

"Michael has a job lined up and I'm transferring to a full-time position at American Airlines in San Francisco."

Finally, "You're not pregnant, are you?"

"No!" Dana replied adamantly.

Finally, after hours of going back and forth, her dad said to Michael, "Welcome to the family."

When Dana finished her story, Jackie sat on the bed stunned. Dana was so happy that she didn't see Jackie's look of concern.

The end of the school year at Wilberforce was a mad rush for both of them; keeping up their GPA's, helping the freshmen students as they faced finals, and going to Cincinnati on weekends to help Dana's mom with the wedding plans. The last week was extremely hard as they said final good-byes to friends and teachers.

The last night they stayed up talking and laughing, looking back at the last two years. There was no way they could have predicted how much their lives would change in the years to come.

"I guess we're closing this chapter and going on to the next one," Jackie said.

Dana thought for a moment, "No, closing the chapter sounds like an end, we're not closing a chapter; we're going to the next phase, the normal progression of life."

Jackie felt honored when Dana asked her to be her maid of honor. In July, 1973, Dana and Michael had a small traditional wedding at St. Martin DePorres Church and a catered reception at the neighborhood community center. Even Gran, who rarely left the state of Virginia, attended. Dana and her family treated her with all the privileges of a grandmother, and they became an extended family. Now Dana's mom called Gran at least once a month and Dana wrote her regularly. Gran told Jackie that this was all new to her because in the past, these types of close relationships were only with family members.

She and Dana continued to stay in close contact. Since Dana worked full time for the airlines and Jackie had a dorm room to herself, Dana usually came to visit her once a year. They arranged visits when she was between semesters. They would act as they had when they first met; staying up all night catching up on things they hadn't shared in their letters. Then they'd top it off by walking Manhattan for blocks and blocks and window shopping. No matter how long they were apart, they always caught up where they left off, as if no time had elapsed.

Now Jackie would be graduating in two weeks and getting married two months later. The New York Knicks drafted Gary immediately after he graduated and he began playing as a rookie back-up. The team management and other players predicted he'd play more and more, as he adjusted to the high level of professionalism in the NBA.

Gary wanted to get married right after he finished college, but Jackie refused to get married until she completed her undergrad degree. A couple of the basketball player's wives had approached her and asked why she didn't want to get married now. "Look, you don't need to have a degree, Gary loves you."

Jackie listened politely and ignored their advice. Dana surprised her when she told her about the pressure she was receiving from other player's wives.

"You're right, don't do it until you finish college. I really love Michael, but I wish we had waited. It looks much easier than it really is. By the time, you work, cook, clean and attend school you're tired so it becomes difficult to study. I am still working on my degree, but I'm not where I planned to be. Now I'm considering changing my major from social work to business administration, so it's going to take even longer."

Jackie looked at her watch. It was 3:00 p.m. and she had been sitting and reminiscing on the park bench for almost two hours. She knew she should be contacting the wedding planner to follow up on the arrangements. Since Gary was such a well- known player, they weren't able to have the type of small wedding she wanted. His agent had secured a top-notch wedding planner so she had very little work to do. Sometimes, she felt like she was watching another person plan their wedding.

*1977*

# Chapter 14

Michael and Dana had recently celebrated their fourth anniversary. When they moved to Oakland, it was exciting for both of them. Everything was fine for the first few years. She was working at the airlines, taking college courses and they traveled frequently. They visited their parents at least once a year. They had even built up a substantial savings.

Michael's parents had stopped drinking, but each had serious health problems. His brother, Aaron, had turned his back on them, so Michael and Dana tried to help them as much as they could. They worked hard to get them get out of their dilapidated apartment and now they lived in a senior citizens complex in downtown Cincinnati.

When they got married, they agreed that Michael would manage the bills because Dana was working and going to school. She didn't have any problem with that arrangement since that was the way her parents dealt with their finances. They deposited their salaries into a joint checking account and Michael paid the bills.

Dana worked nights since she had low seniority. Her first sign that something was wrong was when she awoke one afternoon to go to work and the electricity was off. Since she was in a hurry, she thought there was probably a power outage in the neighborhood so she quickly dressed and left for work. When she arrived home that evening, the power was still off and Michael wasn't home yet, which was unusual. She quickly found some candles, which she was lighting when Michael arrived.

She told him that the power was off when she left for work and she mistakenly thought there was a power outage in the area. There definitely was no power outage in their area since the lights were on throughout the apartment complex. He told her he didn't know what was wrong. Michael attempted to call Pacific Gas and Electric (PG&E) but they were closed so he couldn't get an answer.

Before he left for work the next morning, he woke her and told her he had contacted the power company but they hadn't received their payment. He was going down to their office to pay them cash and the power would be restored later that day.

After that, other small things happened. The phone was disconnected and his excuse was that he had mailed the payment and Oakland's post office must be the worst in the nation. When she went to write a check for groceries, the store contacted the bank to approve the check, but there weren't sufficient funds in the account to cover a $50.00 check. Dana mentioned what was happening to Jackie and she suggested that maybe Dana should take over the finances since she was good at managing money.

When Dana told Michael, she thought it might be a good idea if she began handling the finances he became angry and they had an argument. He accused her of trying to be the man of the house saying, "That sounds like something your high falutin friend Jackie would say." Michael knew that she and Jackie were like sisters, but since Jackie married Gary, Michael always seemed to have a negative comment about her. Dana decided to drop the issue. Shortly after that, Michael started taking their monthly checking account statement with him to work.

One night, when Dana arrived, there was an eviction notice on the door. Michael had come in late again and Dana could smell alcohol on his breath. This time his excuse was that, he hadn't received a bonus check he was expecting.

"The bonus check shouldn't matter, Michael. Between us, we make more than enough money to pay the rent." This only provoked another long and frustrating argument.

"Michael, I can't live like this, with utilities being turned off, going to a grocery store and having a check rejected, and now an eviction notice. I wasn't raised like this. I need to start handling the finances."

They were standing close to each other in the hallway of their apartment and the next thing she knew he was hitting her. He shoved her and then he hit her. She became hysterical; she tried to fight him back but he kept hitting her and screaming at her.

"How dare you try to run this house, if it wasn't for me you'd still be in Ohio?"

She finally got away from him, ran into the hallway bathroom and locked the door. She slumped to the floor, with her back against the door, crying and thinking *what has come over Michael*. He was one of the gentlest people she had ever known. After a while, he came to the door apologizing, swearing that he didn't know what had come over him and that he would never do it again. She stayed in the bathroom all night, using guest towels to wrap around her to stay warm.

The next morning, Michael didn't go to work. He stood at the bathroom door pleading for her to come out, saying he had drunk too much and reiterated he would never do it again. When she finally came out of the bathroom, he could see the marks that he had left on her body and he began to cry.

"I'm sorry, I'm sorry. I will never do this again. I'll pay the rent today and get my act together."

After that, he was back to his gentle self. He continued to take care of the money and she didn't see any more indications that things weren't going well.

In December 1977, she discovered that she was two months pregnant and although it wasn't planned, they both were happy. She was still taking college courses although it was usually only one or two courses per semester during the day. Michael was supportive of her, even doing the laundry and grocery shopping. She noticed that he wasn't getting the name brands he insisted she buy when she did the shopping, but she attributed that to his being frugal since they were expecting a baby.

Shortly after she discovered that she was pregnant, the airlines notified employees that they would relocate their offices to Fort Worth, Texas, the following year. They would offer relocation packages for those interested in moving to Texas or a generous severance plan, which included medical care, for those who chose to remain in the Bay Area. She knew that moving to Texas was not an option for her because she already had too much time invested in getting her degree in California. She thought that with the severance package, she could return to school full-time, but she needed to see how their savings account looked. Usually Michael told her how much money they had in the account so she rarely checked the balance.

She was taking an accounting course, so she decided she would review their finances to determine if they could manage financially with the additional costs for the baby and her not working. She thought it might be rough, but if they used some of the money in the savings account to pay off her car, then they should be okay. She was shocked when she opened the savings passbook and saw that they had less than $300.00 in the account. Michael was withdrawing $15.00 to $25.00 on a regular basis.

She tried to contact him at work, but the assistant manager told her he hadn't come to work. In fact, she was instructed to call his home to see where he was. Dana immediately came up with an excuse and told her that she had forgotten that he had a dental appointment. She took off from work that day and started to go through their financial records. She found the checking statements that Michael had been taking with him hidden in his closet. She discovered that Michael was routinely overdrawing the checking account before they had their argument over the finances and he hit her. After that incident, he left the checking account untouched, but instead began withdrawing money from their savings account.

Since he didn't know she hadn't gone to work that day, he arrived home approximately thirty minutes before she was due to arrive. He went directly into their bedroom, which was close to the front door. She was sitting in the living room, in the dark. From where she was sitting, she could see directly into their bedroom, which was down the hall. She watched as he took off his jacket and threw it on the bed, then reached into his pants pocket and took out a small bag. He stood next to his chest of drawers, opened the top drawer and removed a sheet of white paper. Dana watched in shock as he laid the paper on the dresser, sprinkled white powder from the bag on the paper, lowered his head, placed his finger on his left nostril and inhaled.

She couldn't believe what she was seeing; Michael was snorting coke. He had continued smoking marijuana when they moved to the Bay Area, but she never thought he'd try anything stronger than that.

Still unaware that she was home and watching him, Michael hid the plastic bag under the mattress on his side of the bed. Then he headed into their bathroom and started the shower. When she was sure that he was in the shower, she went to the front door and pretended she was arriving home. He came out of the shower shortly after she entered their bedroom.

"I called you at the restaurant and they told me you hadn't been in all day."

"I was in a training class. The new assistant manager must have forgotten to check the schedule."

Dana had taken an elective course the year before on substance abuse and Michael was exhibiting all of the symptoms: not reporting to work, lying, going through large quantities of money, and irrational behavior like he exhibited the night he hit her. The last thing she was going to do, however, was confront him when he was high. One of the men she worked with was a cocaine addict and when they fired him for poor performance, he punched his supervisor in the face and broke his nose.

The next morning, she told Michael about the impending airline relocation and the offer the company was making. She told him she thought it was a great opportunity for her to spend time with the baby and finish her degree faster than she planned.

Michael listened, but said nothing.

1978

# Chapter 15

When Jackie completed her undergraduate studies, she received a full academic scholarship to Columbia University Law School. Law school was extremely difficult, but she loved it. It was even more exciting than she thought and she was doing exceptionally well in all her classes.

Now she was in her final year and almost finished. She got up early Friday morning to write a paper on ethics for her international tax law class. She wanted to complete the paper before she left on a trip to Philadelphia to recruit for the law school.

It was a cold January morning and while she waited for the coffee to perk, she looked out of their penthouse window and saw that it was snowing. She loved this view of the city, looking at the lights, which were even prettier when it was snowing; like looking at a postcard. She and Gary had been married for over two years and enjoyed a great lifestyle in New York where they lived in a large apartment on the west side of Manhattan close to Central Park. They could easily afford the unit since

Gary's career with the Knicks was going well, with more game time each season.

She poured a cup of coffee and headed to the study to work. As she finished her paper, she looked up and Gary was standing by the door with a cup of coffee in his hand.

"How long have you been up?"

"Since four."

He shook his head, "I don't know how you do it." By now, he was accustomed to waking up and finding her in the study working on an assignment.

They both heard the front door open and knew it was Iris, their housekeeper. Jackie was against having a housekeeper at first; it seemed so pretentious. In fact, she really wasn't comfortable being the wife of a professional basketball player who was constantly in the public eye. She was expected to attend various social functions, be present at home games and run their home. In addition to those responsibilities, she attended law school. She tried to do it all the first few months they were married, but one day while she was talking to Gran she burst into tears. She felt like she wasn't doing anything right.

Gran surprised her when she said, "You need to get some help, someone to clean the house and cook meals."

Jackie was astonished, but before she could say anything Gran continued, "There's nothing wrong with hiring someone to cook and do housework. Pay the person a decent salary, treat them well and your life will be much easier." She followed Gran's advice and now she did not know what she would do without Iris.

They went into the kitchen and said good morning to Iris who was already beginning breakfast.

"I'm surprised to see you up already, Gary," Iris said.

"Well, Jackie is leaving for Philly this afternoon, so I thought I'd spend the morning with her. I have a friend coming to town so I'll probably eat out tonight or we'll get some take out, so you can take the weekend off."

"Sure," Iris responded with a smile, "If you say so."

"Who's visiting," Jackie asked her husband? "I didn't know anyone was coming."

"Oh, I thought I told you, baby. I got a call yesterday from Jarvis Matthews and he's going to be in town so we'll probably hangout. Maybe have some drinks and talk about old times."

Jarvis and Gary were best friends in college, but Jackie hadn't seen him since he and Gary graduated. He was supposed to be in their wedding, but got sick at the last minute.

"How's he doing?"

"He's doing fine; he's a disc jockey for a major radio station in Atlanta."

"Tell him I said hello and to stop being a stranger. I haven't seen him in years."

Jackie was excited about the weekend trip. This was the second year that she had participated in the Columbia recruitment effort. It was always nice when students met her, since many of them could not envision an African American student graduating from Columbia and now attending their law school. She could tell that many of them never considered admittance to an Ivy League college.

She looked at the clock in the kitchen and said, "It's almost ten o'clock. I need to finish packing so I can make the noon train to Philadelphia."

She was packed and ready to go in an hour. She gave Gary a kiss and said, "See you Sunday evening. The sessions will be over on Saturday, but we decided to work on the assessment while we're all together since we're traveling from so many areas of the country."

"No problem, Iris will be off so we can order take out when you return."

"I should be home by six Sunday night. Make it Chinese and you've got a deal." He walked her to the door and she gave him a hug before heading to the elevator.

She was looking forward to the train ride to Philadelphia. She loved the trains on the East Coast and used them whenever she could. It was partially because she and Gran had taken a train ride when she was little and she had fond memories of their trip, and because it was so relaxing. After she boarded, she immediately closed her eyes and was asleep before the train pulled out of the station.

She had slept only a short period; awakened by the voices of two women who had come in and sat directly behind her.

One of the women was saying, "Valerie, you need to get a sex therapist."

Jackie heard the other woman respond, "I can't do that. You know John is not going to go to any type of shrink."

"That's exactly what Charles said until I convinced him it would improve our sex life."

"Well...maybe I'll try it. I certainly didn't plan to get married at thirty and have such a dismal sex life."

As she listened to the women talking, Jackie thought, *maybe she and Gary needed a sex therapist.* They had been married for over two years, but Jackie was puzzled at how their relationship was evolving. From the outside, it appeared they had the perfect marriage. Gary was attentive and generous to a fault. When he was on a road trip, he always came home with an expensive gift for her. Somehow, marriage didn't feel the way she had imagined it would; she and Gary were more like good friends than husband and wife.

One of the things that bothered her was that they rarely had sex. She had beautiful lingerie and she dressed provocatively at night, but she was seldom able to entice him. She heard the other player's wives talk and they all seemed to have exciting sex lives.

Once when she broached the subject with Gary, he became irritated and said, "Jackie I'm sorry, I've never been that interested in sex. I've played basketball since I was a teenager and there was always this talk about being careful; not to fool around or have sex before a game. I guess I've taken it too far."

Jackie didn't feel comfortable discussing their marriage problems with anyone, not even Dana. As she overheard the women talking, she decided to locate a sex therapist as soon as possible.

The recruitment session went extremely well, so when she returned to her hotel suite, she continued to think about the conversation she overheard on the train. She reached for the phone to call Gary, but decided this was a matter best discussed in person. Gary would be on the road next week, so she wanted to talk with him about contacting a sex therapist before he left. She thought he might resist at first, but a week on the road would give him time to get used to the idea.

Later Jackie tried to reach Gary a couple of times, to let him know she arrived safely, but there was no answer. She figured he and Jarvis were out having a good time. She knew Jarvis would be leaving around noon on Sunday and if she got home Saturday evening, she would have an opportunity to see him. The session ended at seven the next night and Jackie decided to leave that night when the other presenters expressed a desire to do their assessment via phone the next week.

She arrived home around 11:00 that evening. She figured Gary wouldn't be in since Jarvis was in town, so she planned to go in, take a shower and surprise him when he got home.

When she opened the door, she could hear the stereo playing. The apartment was dark, but she could see a faint light emitting from their bedroom so she walked toward their bedroom door, which was partially open. She started to call Gary's name, but heard a strange sound. She stopped, not sure exactly what the sound was. As she pushed the door open, she heard Gary say, "I love you, Jarvis. I love you, man."

Then she saw Gary and Jarvis on the bed naked with Gary on top, making love. With the music in the background and their loud moaning, they had no idea she was standing at the door until she screamed.

Gary jumped up and looked toward the door, and for a fleeting moment, their eyes met. Jackie stood there in shock, tears streaming down her face, saying "No, No." She heard Gary say, "Damn," as he quickly reached for his pants, which were lying next to the bed, and headed toward her.

He approached her and reached out to touch her. She instinctively drew back. She knew that she didn't want him to ever put his hands on her again. She screamed, "I hate you," and quickly turned and ran down the hallway and out the door; leaving her suitcase by the door. In the background she could hear Gary calling, "Jackie. Wait….I'm sorry, Jackie. Let me try to explain."

When she reached the elevator, she didn't know what she was going to do or where she was going to go. She knew she wanted to get as far away from Gary as possible. She pressed the button for the lobby, leaned against the wall and as the door closed, she retched and threw up on the elevator floor. When the elevator reached the lobby and the door opened, she saw her reflection in the elevator mirror. Knowing she couldn't go into the lobby looking the way she did; crying, the smell of vomit on her, mascara running, she pressed the button for the garage thinking, *I'll get the car and drive somewhere where I can think.*

As she got out of the elevator and approached their car, she decided to check into a hotel. She realized that she had left her suitcase in the apartment. She went to the trunk of the car and removed her gym bag, which she always kept stocked with toiletries and a change of casual clothes. She took the elevator back to the lobby, went to the visitor's bathroom and cleaned up, then exited the building from the side door and hailed a taxi to a small hotel in midtown.

After she checked in and went to her room, she went over the scene of Gary and Jarvis making love and it made her sick again. She rushed to the bathroom and threw up, then sat on the bathroom floor wondering, *what am I going to do?*

When she came out of the bathroom, she reached for the phone and called Dana.

Dana answered on the second ring and immediately knew something was wrong.

"Jackie, what is it? Is something wrong with Gran?"

"No, Gran is fine."

"Then what is it, I can tell that you're crying. By the way, where are you? Are you still in Philly?"

"No," said Jackie, "I decided to come home early."

Then she told Dana what happened. Dana was quiet as she spoke. Jackie finished by telling her that she had checked into a hotel.

"Wow, I can't believe this; Gary and Jarvis!"

"We've never had a very good sex life and I came home early so I could suggest that we see a sex therapist. I thought if we got help, it would improve the relationship, but now I definitely know that's not going to happen. Not only were they making love, but I heard Gary tell Jarvis he loved him. I'm sorry to bother you with this, but I needed to talk to someone before I go crazy. Now I feel guilty, you have enough on your plate with your own marital problems."

"Don't worry about me; we're friends and that's what friends are for. What do you want to do? Do you want to get away? Maybe come out and stay with me for a while?"

"No, I can't. I have papers due this week."

After much discussion, they decided that Dana would change her work schedule and catch a flight to New York the following weekend.

"I need to get away too," said Dana. "Will you be okay until I get there?"

"I guess I'll be all right. Gary has to leave Monday morning so I'll be able to go to the apartment and get my clothes then."

"I'll call you before I go to work tomorrow," Dana said, before hanging up.

When Jackie finished talking to Dana she headed for the shower. When she came out of the shower, it dawned on her that she did not have any pajamas so she wrapped herself in the hotel bathrobe, which was hanging in the closet. She lay across the bed trying to sleep, but couldn't. She thought about the fact that she rarely saw Jarvis after she and Gary began dating. Prior to that Gary and Jarvis had been very close friends, always together. Now she knew why Jarvis failed to attend their wedding. Finally, she fell asleep.

When she awoke, she thought she was coming out of a bad dream. She saw her clothes strewn around the room and she knew she hadn't been dreaming. Everything she saw and heard the night before came quickly back. She had a horrible headache, so she called room service and ordered breakfast and asked them to bring her some aspirin.

It was 9:00 a.m. so she gave Gran a call. She didn't think Gary would call her, but she wanted to make sure. They spoke briefly and Gran told her she would be at church all day since this was the Sunday for the women's annual tea. Gran asked her when she would return to New York and Jackie told her probably not until Monday since the team had more work to complete than they originally thought. She hated lying, but she was not ready to tell Gran what happened, not right now.

She had so many questions she wanted to ask Gary; first, why? Based on what she saw and heard, he was really in love with Jarvis and probably had been for a long time before they were married. Why did he get married in the first place and drag her into it?

She wrapped the covers around her and the tears began again. She must have cried herself to sleep because she didn't awake until the phone rang. It was Dana, who told her Gary had just called asking if she had heard from Jackie. When she hesitated he said, "Look, Dana, I know you guys are like sisters so you probably won't tell me the truth, but if you talk to her, please ask her to call me. I will be home all day. Please tell her I am so sorry. I never meant to hurt her. If she doesn't want to talk to me, I'll understand. Let her know that I'll be leaving on Monday."

When Dana finished, she asked, "Do you want to talk to him?"

"No."

Then she told Dana that she realized that Gary's relationship with Jarvis had probably been going on when they were in college, but she was too blind to see it.

"No, Jackie, I've known Gary as long as you have and I didn't see it either. There definitely were no obvious signs." They talked for a while and Dana said she had to go to work, but would check on her when she got off.

# Chapter 16

Jackie left the hotel at 8:00 Monday morning. She knew Gary would be on the 7:00 a.m. flight so she wasn't worried about running into him. She wasn't sure how she would react when she went back into the apartment so she wanted to arrive before Iris did. When she turned the key in the lock all the memories came rushing back. She walked into the apartment and it was very bright. Gary had left all the blinds open. When she got to the bedroom door her legs almost buckled, but she kept walking into the living room and sat on the couch. She opened her purse and took out her list of things to do that she made the previous night. At the top of the list was to get an attorney. She planned to file for divorce immediately.

When Iris arrived, Jackie asked her to pack all her clothes. She had already taken her luggage out and got a few boxes that were in the basement storage area. Iris was like a mother figure to Jackie and Gary so she knew something was seriously wrong, but she could tell from Jackie's demeanor that this was not the time to ask. Jackie was not sure where she was going to live, but it definitely would not be with Gary. For right now, she would stay at the hotel temporarily.

Jackie left the apartment, dropped her clothes off at the hotel and headed directly to the law school. She planned to check the student bulletin board for a place to stay. There were always notices on the board for apartments to sublet. She immediately saw two signs that sounded interesting, and more importantly, were close to the law school. Since Monday was a light class day, she was able to schedule appointments to view both units later that afternoon. She decided to take a small studio since it was available immediately and within walking distance of the school. By Wednesday evening, she had all her personal items in the studio and stayed there for the night. She called Gran that evening and told her everything including the fact that she would be filing for divorce the next day.

Gran was quiet at first, then asked, "Are you sure that's what you want to do right now?"

"Gran, I want this to be over. It's clear that he's in love with someone else. If it were a woman, I might be able to compete, but not with a man."

"Have you talked to Gary yet?"

"No," said Jackie. "He's left messages with Iris asking me to call, but I won't call him."

"I can understand that. I know you are hurting, but don't let that hurt have you do something that might ruin him for the rest of his life. Gary has always been a kind person. Remember that it's not always what you do, but how you do it."

Before they hung up, Gran said, "I love you, baby, I know you'll do what's right."

After she got off the phone, she thought about her conversation with Gran. Yes, she was angry and hurt, but she definitely did not want to divulge her personal business. She also knew that in pro sports Gary's career might be ruined if there were ever an inkling of his sexual preference. She was in her last semester of law school and she knew it would be one of the tougher ones. *Do I really want to go through a divorce now?*

On Thursday, she met with John Petersen, the attorney she decided to retain to handle her divorce. Jackie had worked with John last summer as his law clerk at a prestigious Manhattan firm. She enjoyed working with him and decided to have him represent her, because he was very family oriented and she knew he would be discreet. Recently he opened his own office, specializing in family law.

She was surprised when she arrived at the relatively small, although professional office with a reception area and one secretary.

When John came out to meet her, he said, "A little bit different from my old office."

"Yes, but very nice."

He escorted her into his office and they made small talk for a while, talking about people John stayed in contact with from his previous firm. He told her he enjoyed having his own practice, since he was now able to get home most evenings and have dinner with his family. He was surprised when she told him she wanted to file for legal separation now and would file for divorce when she completed law school.

"Do you mind me asking why?"

John met Gary at a summer office party when Jackie worked for him and they had hit it off well, so she expected him to be curious as to why the divorce

Jackie replied, "Irreconcilable differences."

John said, "Okay. Understood, but I do need to ask another question. Do I need to get a restraining order?"

"No, Gary isn't violent, I'll be fine."

She was devastated, but she remembered what Gran told her about not ruining his life. When she was growing up, Gran always said, "What happens in this house stays in this house."

Right now, all she needed to do was to be away from Gary and concentrate on finishing law school. She wanted a monthly allowance to cover her expenses until June.

John took all the information and said that he would file the papers for legal separation on Friday and have Gary served with legal notice when he returned to New York.

By the time Jackie met Dana's flight Friday afternoon, she was exhausted. In six days, she had submitted all her assignments, found an apartment to sublet until June, moved all of her clothes out of the apartment and filed for legal separation. As long as she stayed busy she didn't think about her failing marriage or what she witnessed Saturday night.

She met Dana at the airline gate and when she saw her, she thought, *oh, my god, she really is pregnant*. Dana had called her as soon as she found out, but seeing her was entirely different. She was so pretty, with a glow to her skin. Her stomach was slightly rounded and she was wearing a cute red jumper and turtleneck.

"Dana, you look so pretty."

"Oh sure I do," Dana laughed. "Look how big I am. I swear I lost my waistline the moment I got pregnant. The next thing that goes in pregnancy are your pants. I've already outgrown all of them."

As soon as they got to Jackie's place, they began talking and Jackie quickly brought Dana up to date. She called Dana when she got the apartment to give her the new telephone number, but she hadn't told her about meeting with an attorney.

When Jackie finished, Dana said, "At least you'll have money to complete law school."

"Yes, that's what I was really concerned about. I'm on an academic scholarship, which covers my tuition and books, with a small amount left, but definitely not enough to cover an apartment. I saved some money when I worked last summer, but I used most of that to pay the deposit and first month's rent on this apartment. I checked the campus bulletin board and there were a few part-time jobs listed that might work with my schedule, so I submitted applications this week. It's going to be a demanding schedule, but I need to stay busy now."

"I don't know how I didn't see this. When I look back there were signs, he and Jarvis always meeting when I was away, his lack of sex drive, but somehow I didn't equate them with what I saw last Saturday night."

They continued talking until the wee hours when they both began yawning and called it a night.

When they awoke the next morning and looked out of the window, it was pouring down rain. They decided to remain in their pajamas and called a nearby restaurant to deliver breakfast.

During breakfast, Jackie said, "You haven't said much about Michael. Is he excited about the baby?"

"I don't know. Michael's changed a lot in the last year or so." She looked away before continuing, "Remember when I told you about his mismanaging our money?"

"Yeah, I thought you were going to begin handling the money."

"I tried to, but that didn't work. He accused me of trying to take over his role. When I received official notice that

American Airlines would begin relocating in June, I checked our savings account balance and we only had about $300.00 in the account."

"I thought you were working hard to save money for a house, what happened?"

"This is much worse than I told you; Michael is seriously hooked on coke."

"Wow!" exclaimed Jackie.

Dana told her she had attempted to discuss the drug issue with him, but he denied it. "Last year he started getting home later and later. On three occasions, he didn't come home at all, using the excuse that some equipment broke at the restaurant. He said he had to stay until they could get a repairperson to come out and fix the problem. He started missing work in the fall. Last month I got a call from his manager who was looking for him. He asked me to tell him not to bother coming back to work. When I told him he shrugged it off, saying he and the new owner weren't getting along well, and he planned to quit anyway."

"Then he told me, 'You make enough money, we'll be okay until I get a new job.' He leaves the house early every day saying he's going out looking for a job, but I think he's lying. I'm beginning to miss things around the apartment. Michael had an expensive gold chain that I haven't seen since he lost his job. The gold bracelet that my parents gave me for my 18$^{th}$ birthday is also missing. I think he sold them or pawned them."

Jackie asked, "Why didn't you tell me everything?"

"I've been trying to work this out. When I heard American was relocating to Texas, I was happy. I thought we had enough money saved, and with the severance package and unemployment, I'd be able to return to college full-time. Last week I found out, I won't qualify for unemployment if I'm a full-time student. I had even arranged for an older woman at my church to take care of the baby. Now I don't know what I'm going to do."

Jackie sighed, "How did we get here, with two worthless ass husbands? We're only twenty four and neither one of us deserves this kind of mess."

Dana admitted that she still loved Michael, but knew she didn't want to stay with him any longer with his drug addiction. She had considered moving back to Ohio with her parents, but she wanted to finish her degree, and changing colleges would prolong that. In addition, the cost of education in California was extremely reasonable. As of now, she didn't have any student loans, and she didn't want to incur any. They weighed the pros and cons of various options, each had their pluses and minuses.

Suddenly, Jackie said, "Wait a minute, what if I move out to California? We can get an apartment together, and I can help you with the baby until you finish college?"

Dana said, "What? No, I appreciate what you're trying to do, but I got in this mess by myself and I'll figure a way to get out of it."

"No. Think about it. This can work out for both of us. I am not going to want to stay in New York when my divorce is final. Most of the friends I have are due to Gary and his position. Once I finish law school, I can leave New York and get away from Gary. The baby is due in July and I'm not planning to work this summer. I can help you until you get back on your feet. Then I'll begin studying for the bar exam."

They continued going back and forth and Dana finally agreed that it might work. They figured that if they combined their monies, they would be able to get an apartment in May and Jackie could move to the Bay Area as soon as she graduated in June. Dana would find an apartment close to the bus line so that she wouldn't have to drive to San Francisco State University (SFSU) when she enrolled. Since she changed her major from social work to business, she only had a few more courses at the junior college and she would complete them soon. They stayed up through the night making a detailed plan of what they had to do. Dana wasn't sure what she was going to tell Michael, but she decided she'd handle that when she got ready to leave him.

# Chapter 17

When she returned to the Bay Area, Dana began having second thoughts about leaving Michael. Driving across the Bay Bridge, she wondered whether she was doing the right thing by planning to leave, maybe she should give him an opportunity to change, maybe a little more time. She knew she still loved him. She thought about their baby that she was carrying and she knew she didn't want to raise their child alone. So far, she had only told Jackie about Michael's drug problem, maybe she needed to look into getting him into some type of drug rehabilitation program.

She knew that Marsha, an older co-worker of hers, husband had been on drugs for years. Marsha got him into a program and he had been clean for over ten years. She decided to talk with Marsha and get some information from her. Maybe with some help, Michael could get off drugs and they could turn their marriage around.

When she arrived home, she planned to talk to Michael about their relationship. He was in the living room lying on the couch watching a football game. The Sunday newspaper was sprawled on the floor in front of him. Somehow, she knew they were going to have an argument by the way he looked at her when she entered the room. Even without him speaking, she could tell he was angry. He knew she had been to visit Jackie so his first question was, "Did you and your uppity friend have a good weekend?"

She answered, "She's not uppity and yes we did have a nice weekend. It was good seeing her and catching up."

He continued, "I don't know how you think we can afford for you to fly to New York when I'm not working. We could have used that money to pay rent."

"You know I used my flight benefits, so there was no cost."

"Well, why do you have those bags with you, if you didn't spend any money?"

"Jackie bought these for the baby."

"Yeah, right," said Michael.

Then he said, "I need some money."

"I don't have any money, Michael. I don't get paid until Friday so I only have enough money for gas and lunch next week."

He sat up and quickly grabbed her purse that she had laid on the coffee table, which was directly in front of him.

"What are you doing?" she asked. "Don't touch my purse."

She got up from the chair she was sitting in and walked toward him to grab her purse from him. As she approached him, he stood up and held her purse above his head so she couldn't reach it and said, "Well, since you had a good weekend, I think I'll do the same."

When she attempted to get her purse from him again, he pushed her and she fell backwards into the chair. *You're pregnant,*

*don't fight him back, there's only $25 in your purse, let him have it.*
He rummaged through her purse, found the money, grabbed
it and threw the purse on the floor. He slammed the door as
he walked out of the apartment and he didn't come home that
night.

The next day she sought Marsha out at work and asked
her if she was free for lunch. When they met she told her
everything about Michael, his not coming home, his being
fired from work, missing jewelry, seeing him snorting coke, the
altercation they had a few months ago, and how he had taken
her money yesterday.

Marsha let her talk before asking, "Are you okay? Do you
need any money?"

"No, I always keep a $20 bill in a hidden compartment of
my wallet and some money in the glove compartment of my car
so I have enough money until pay day."

Dana asked Marsha if she knew of a place where Michael
could get help.

Marsha responded, "There are many organizations that help
addicts, but Michael would need to initiate it." She continued,
"Dana, when people are hooked on drugs, you can't help them
until they acknowledge that they have a problem. Sometimes
that can take years and sometimes it never happens. You know
that my husband, Paul, is no longer on drugs, but very few
people know how long it was before he got help. I was in denial
just as he was for years. I was always making excuses for him.
I wouldn't acknowledge that he seldom worked and that I was
carrying all of the responsibility."

"One day, I attended church and they had a sermon on co-
dependency, and I realized that I was as bad as he was. No, I
didn't use drugs, but I allowed him to continue using with my
excuses and my acceptance. I joined a support group and finally

gave Paul an ultimatum, get help with your drug problem or I'm leaving you, and I eventually left him. He finally got help, but it wasn't until he almost died from an overdose that he even acknowledged he was an addict. He finally went to a rehab program, but he relapsed twice before he got clean. We now have a nonprofit organization to help family members of addicts, and I'd like to have you come to our next meeting."

The following weekend Dana attended the meeting, which was held in a conference room at Marsha's church. There was a variety of people in attendance: some old and some young, parents, spouses, and people of various cultures. Each of them shared a common problem; someone they loved was addicted to drugs. One parent spoke about tough love. She no longer allowed her son to come to her home. She cried saying, "I never thought there'd be a day when I would not allow my child to enter my home." As Dana listened to people speak, she began to realize that Michael was much worse than she thought.

After the meeting, Dana told Marsha about the plan for Jackie to move to California. Marsha listened and then said, "I'm glad that you have a plan, and even more so, a friend that will provide support to you now. You know Paul and I don't have children; I think if we did, I would have left him much sooner. I definitely would not have wanted to raise children in the environment I lived in with him for all those years."

Before they left, she gave Dana her business card with her home phone number on the back, and said, "You can call me anytime."

When she got home, Michael wasn't there. She could tell that he had been in the apartment because he left a pile of dirty clothes in the bathroom. That night as she lay in bed, she realized that if Michael got himself together, she'd be there for him, but right now, her priority was she and her baby.

The next day, she decided to eat lunch before she left for work. In order to get to the kitchen in their apartment, you had to go through the living room. As she walked through the living room, something seemed different. Initially she shrugged her shoulders; it was probably because she rarely went in the kitchen before she left for work. Then it dawned on her. *Where is Michael's stereo equipment?* She walked back into the living room; the two large speakers, plus a turntable and various other pieces of stereo equipment, which he had acquired over the years, were all gone.

She went to the door, grabbed the newspaper and immediately turned to the classified section. She found the rental section and began circling a few apartments that looked interesting, ones, which she and Jackie should be able to afford. During her lunch hour, she began making calls. She was surprised at how many apartment complexes would not take children or pets. Later that day, she spoke to Jackie and jokingly told her, "I'm not sure what they think is worse, children or pets." She was glad she started looking early because it looked like it was going to be more difficult than she thought.

Jackie told her that Gary agreed to the separation and a sizable amount for monthly spousal support. She was still looking for a job since she felt better when she was busy. Right now, she was volunteering by tutoring first year law students. She acknowledged that it was hard being alone in the small studio apartment at night.

Dana told Jackie about the support group and that she planned to continue attending. She didn't mention the episode with Michael taking money from her purse or the missing stereo equipment.

In March, she arrived home from work one evening and found an eviction notice on their apartment door. There was a padlock on the door so there was no way for her to enter. She stood in front of the door in disbelief, thinking, *what am I going to do?* She had been paying the rent each month; leaving the check with Michael to drop off at the rental office. This must be a mistake, but right now the office was closed and she needed a place to stay. She thought about a hotel, but Michael had "maxed out" their credit cards. She remembered the card that Marsha had given her with her home phone number on it and went to a phone booth and called her. Marsha told her to come to her home and gave her directions. When she got there, Marsha had made a pot of herbal tea and had her sit in a chair with an ottoman where she could rest her feet. As she told her about the eviction notice, she began to cry.

Marsha listened to her and said, "You can stay here. I made the guest room up and I put one of my gowns in there for you. Right now, I want you to go bed and get some rest; this definitely is not good for you or the baby. You can deal with this tomorrow."

When Dana awoke the next morning, she was disoriented, but then everything came back, the eviction notice, coming to Marsha's home. As she looked around the room to locate a phone to call the apartment office, she noticed a rattan chair next to the bed with the clothes she had worn yesterday cleaned and neatly folded. There was a note on top from Marsha that read, *There's plenty of food in the kitchen, please make yourself at home. I'll be back by ten.*

Dana quickly got up, showered and dressed. She fixed a cup of tea and a plain bagel before she called Nina, the manager at her apartment complex. Nina informed her that they were ninety days in arrears with the rent and that they had sent a certified letter regarding the imminent eviction, which Michael signed. *How could this be happening when she had written a check each month for the rent?* She told Nina that she would stop by later that day to make payment arrangements.

She had her checkbook register with her so she contacted the bank. She gave Mrs. Lee, the bank representative, the check numbers for the checks that she had written for the rent and none of them had been cashed. Mrs. Lee was very helpful and said, "Let me look a little closer at your account. Can you give me a number where I can contact you?"

Dana was sitting at the kitchen table looking at the newspaper and searching for an apartment when Marsha got home. Last week she had located an apartment for her and Jackie, but it wouldn't be available until early in May. She needed an apartment now. She was giving Marsha an update when the phone rang. Marsha answered and handed it to her.

Mrs. Lee said that she had examined her checking account and on the first day of each month, Michael cashed a counter check for $575.00. She offered to get a copy of the checks for her if she needed them. Dana thanked her, but told her that wouldn't be necessary. She knew what had happened.

When she got off the phone, she told Marsha what Mrs. Lee had told her. She went on to tell her how she had opened a checking account last year, which she used primarily for personal items. When Michael lost his job, she began depositing her paycheck in that account instead of their joint account, but rarely balanced the checkbook. Michael knew she wouldn't look at the cancelled checks, so he cashed a counter check at the first of each month in the exact amount of the rent.

When she finished, she began to cry, then she stopped, wiped her eyes and told Marsha, "No, I'm tired of crying. I've been crying for over a year. The only person Michael is interested in is Michael; he doesn't give a damn about me or our baby. Not only did he steal the rent money, but he signed a certified letter that contained the eviction notice, knowing damn well we would be put out on the street."

She told Marsha that she needed to go and take care of some business. Marsha said, "Dana, you're upset, and you should be, but if you don't mind, why don't I go with you?"

Marsha drove and their first stop was the bank, where Dana removed Michael's name from her checking account. While she was there, she closed their joint savings account, which only had a $20 balance. Next, they went to the apartment complex. As they drove, she and Marsha discussed the best way to handle the situation. Marsha said, from her experience, the best way was to be honest. She definitely did not have $2,000 for the late rent and all the legal fees needed to get the apartment back. Nina was very nice after she explained what happened. She said she felt something was wrong, but each time she came by the apartment Michael was home and assured her he would pay the rent.

Nina was lenient and removed the padlock from the apartment door so Dana could go inside and get some clothes and toiletries. She was shocked when she entered the apartment; Michael knew the date of the eviction notice, so he had cleaned out all the things he could carry out of the apartment. Marsha helped her pack her clothes and Nina padlocked the door behind them as they left.

On the way back to her house, Marsha offered to allow her to stay with her and Paul until she could get on her feet. "This is a lot to handle. You're pregnant and you don't need to be by yourself now."

When she got back to Marsha's home, she called her parents and told them everything. Her Mom's immediate response was, "Dana, you need to come home. You're twenty five hundred miles away from us, pregnant, and you don't have any family out there."

"Mom, I'll be okay. I wanted to call to give you and Dad a phone number where you can reach me. I don't need to move, not now"

Her father was on the other phone line and had been quiet the entire time, but he spoke up now. "How much is due on the rent?" he asked.

She said, "No, Dad, I'll handle it."

Then he changed his tone and said, "How much is due, I don't want you or your things put out on the street."

She said, "$2,000."

He said, "I need the address where you're staying and we'll send the money first thing in the morning."

All she could say was, "Thank you."

Then he said, "May I speak to the woman you're staying with?"

She was on the kitchen phone and Marsha was at the stove preparing a late lunch. When she handed her the phone, she smiled. As she sat at the table, she could hear Marsha assuring her dad that she and Paul would take excellent care of her. Finally, Marsha said, "You don't need to thank me, if I had a daughter, I'd want someone to do the same for me."

Dana spoke to her parents again and thanked them profusely. Her dad said, "Take care of yourself and my grandbaby."

# Chapter 18

The next week Dana received two cashier's checks from her parents. One was payable to the apartment complex for the outstanding rent and the other for $1,000 for her and the baby. The attached note read, *We don't want our first grandchild to be without anything.*

She was so happy; a huge weight lifted off her. She paid the delinquent rent and Nina allowed her to terminate the lease. She no longer trusted Michael and she did not want to stay there any longer. She arranged to return the following weekend to empty the apartment. She needed some more personal items, so Nina escorted her to the apartment and removed the padlock. As she turned to leave, she said, "Take your time, technically the apartment is yours now."

She hadn't planned to be in the apartment more than a few minutes, but when Nina left, she sat on the couch in the living room and looked around. She thought about how excited she and Michael were when they first moved to the Bay Area. She looked at the remaining things in the apartment that they had acquired over the past few years; not a lot of things, but things they enjoyed. Then she went into the bedroom, looked around briefly, and gathered the rest of her personal items. As she left the apartment, she knew it was the end of her relationship with Michael.

Marsha and Paul treated her like a daughter. Each day when she awoke, Marsha had breakfast prepared, and in the evenings, she would fix her a hot cup of tea. Although Marsha had nieces and nephews, she had never been around anyone who was pregnant for any length of time. She was like a mother hen.

On the day of the move, Paul got a few teenage boys from their church to come to the apartment and pack, but Marsha was adamant that she was not to lift a finger. They arranged to store her furniture and remaining items in their basement, until her apartment became available in May. As everyone scurried around packing, it occurred to her that she was glad that she had spent time in the apartment by herself earlier in the week. Now the move wasn't emotional to her, it was just a move.

Dana and Jackie talked weekly and both were excited about living together. Dana had taken pictures of the apartment and mailed them to Jackie. It had a roommate floor plan so Jackie's bedroom and bathroom would be on the opposite side of the apartment from Dana and the baby. They agreed to use the remaining furniture from Dana's apartment so they wouldn't have to spend money buying furniture and Jackie would take care of any accessories.

Dana wondered where Michael was. It seemed as if he'd disappeared off the face of the earth. She contacted a couple of his friends, but they hadn't seen him in months. One of them told her that Michael had borrowed money from him and he hadn't seen him since.

Although she wanted the relationship to be over or at least over until Michael could get straight, she missed him. He had been her friend for a long time. When the baby kicked, she wanted him with her to experience that miracle, but she knew she had to accept the fact that, for him, drugs were his priority now.

One evening, after work, she and Marsha were walking to Marsha's car when she heard Michael call her name. When she looked around, he was standing a few feet from her. His clothes were dirty and with the slight bay breeze, she detected a foul body odor.

For a moment, they stared at each other; then he began talking, apologizing and saying he was trying to get his life together.

"Can I borrow a few dollars for food?"

She reached for her purse, then stopped. She could hear the stories of people in the support group running through her head. Family members asking for food money, swearing they were going to change, but continuing the same behavior.

"Michael, I will buy you some food, but I won't give you any money."

"No, you're pregnant and you're with someone; I'll take the money and go get some food."

She wanted so badly for him to say yes, get me some food, but when he turned down her offer, she knew it was a junkie's ploy to get money for drugs. She turned away from him and headed to the car. Then she stopped, turning toward him again.

"Michael, you're not supposed to be in this parking lot. If you show up again, I'll call security. You've made some bad choices, but I'm not going to have my life turned upside down any longer because of you. When you get clean call me; if not, I don't ever want to see you again."

When she got in the car, she sat in her seat shaking, taking deep breaths.

Marsha asked, "Are you okay?"

"Yes, I'm fine." She told her she wanted so badly for Michael to accept the offer for food that she was actually praying. "I'm so happy that I've been attending the support group meetings because without those weekly meetings and stories, I probably would have given him the money."

Marsha said, "I'm so proud of you. I wish I had had that kind of strength when I was dealing with Paul and his addiction."

Dana replied, "I made a decision that I am not getting caught up in what can become a vicious cycle, supporting a junkie, always praying and hoping they he will get clean. I wasn't sure if I could do it. I still love him, but seeing him was like looking at a stranger. I know that I don't want my child to be involved in his world and that alone gave me the strength to say no."

At the next support group, she shared her encounter with Michael with the members and thanked them. "Without your stories and your ongoing support, I probably wouldn't have been able to do it." At the end of the session she was mentally and physically exhausted; she felt like she had gone through a wringer.

The next night Jackie called and Dana told her about seeing Michael and refusing to give him money. As they were talking, Dana glanced at a calendar on the nightstand in her room and saw that Jackie had a little over a month before her graduation from law school. They had spent so much time talking about the baby, Michael, Gary, and Jackie's move to the West Coast that they hadn't talked about her graduation recently.

When Dana brought up the topic, Jackie said, "I didn't originally plan to participate in the graduation exercises."

"Are you crazy?"

"No, I'm not, and don't worry. I told Gran and she set me straight right away."

She said, "We don't have anyone in our family with a law degree, so we can't afford for you not to walk across that stage."

"I realized that this is a big event for her and I owe it to her, and to me, to walk across the stage. I'll start sending out invitations next week."

"I wish I were able to attend, but it's not such a great idea for a woman almost seven months pregnant to fly across country unless it's a dire emergency."

At the beginning of May, Dana moved into the new apartment, a bright, sunny place in the Lake Merritt area of Oakland. From the living room, she could see the lake and the surrounding shops. It would also be great for commuting to school since the bus lines were two blocks away.

Jackie arrived in early June and they spent the first two nights staying up late and talking. Jackie filled her in on her graduation. She was so happy that Dana's parents attended. They had taken her, Gran and Aunt Mildred to a five star restaurant for dinner to celebrate.

Dana's last day at work for American Airlines was June 15, 1978. Marsha decided to take the relocation package and move to Texas, so she and Paul would be leaving in two weeks. That evening, Marsha surprised her with a huge baby shower. She had purchased a crib, car seat, and bassinet with some of the money her parents sent. She planned to get the remaining items her first week off work, but thanks to her co-workers and friends, now she didn't need to do any shopping.

She spent the next few weeks around the apartment, resting and reading. Her feet began to swell, so she only had one pair of shoes to wear, and it was increasingly difficult to move. Sleeping at night was also difficult since she couldn't find a comfortable position. She was seeing her doctor weekly and everything was okay, but Dana was nervous and scared; wondering what labor was going to be like. She had read books on pregnancy and labor, but it was still difficult to envision exactly what to expect. One of her friends told her about her first child's birth and it sounded like she had gone through sheer hell.

One night she awoke to go to the bathroom and when she entered the bathroom, she felt a gush of water from her body. Based on her readings, she knew her water had broken. Since she didn't have any pain, she cleaned up, went to Jackie's room and told her what happened, and asked her to call the doctor. When she got off the phone, she said, "It's time for you to go to the hospital."

While Jackie was getting dressed, she called her parents, gave them the news, telling them Jackie would keep them posted. Jackie stayed with her during labor, which began shortly after she arrived at the hospital. She held her hands, coached her with her breathing, and gave her the support she needed when she was so exhausted she didn't think she could push any more.

Dana had decided that if the baby were a girl she would name her after her grandmothers and she combined their maiden names, Fannie Ash and Bessie Lee. After her final push, Jackie was one of the first to hear Ashlee Marie Adams cry.

# Chapter 19

When Dana arrived home from the hospital with Ashlee, she was anxious. She had never been around infants for more than a couple of hours and although she had read numerous baby books, it wasn't the same. Her parents came out to help, but they could only stay for a week. Gradually, she learned how to breast feed, change diapers quickly with one hand, keep Ashlee relatively clean and well dressed in her adorable new baby clothes, and live pretty much on a few hours of sleep each day.

Jackie spent her mornings studying for the bar exam, but she took a long break in the afternoon to watch Ashlee, allowing Dana time to take a nap. Between the two of them, they established a routine and things began to go smoothly after the first month. No one told Dana how much work there would be, but she enjoyed every moment of it. Ashlee was a beautiful baby. She had mocha skin, the prettiest dark brown eyes and her face lit up when she smiled.

She did not plan to work after Ashlee was born since she expected the severance package to cover a year of living expenses. When she received the check she was shocked; with taxes withheld it was nowhere near what she had expected. Her living expenses soared with the cost of diapers and other necessities; quickly depleting her savings. She wasn't attending college full time yet so she was eligible for unemployment, but even that wasn't enough for her to pay all of her expenses.

By the time Ashlee was five months old, Dana knew she had to return to work so she got a job at a travel agency. Jackie took care of Ashlee the nights she attended school, but college was a slow process with her again only taking one or two courses each semester.

Dana began getting severe headaches and when she went to her physician he told her that based on the extreme pain behind her left eye and nausea, she was experiencing migraines. He asked her about her lifestyle and Dana told him she was estranged from her husband, raising her young daughter, working and attending college at night.

The doctor smiled at her. "You have a great deal of things happening in your life right now. The migraines are probably due to stress, but unfortunately, there is no medication for migraines. Try to find ways to let up a little. That may reduce the stress, but I realize that will be difficult for you right now."

When she got home that afternoon, Dana told Jackie what the doctor had said. Then she said, "Marsha called me last week and I told her what was happening. She suggested that I apply for welfare so I can quit work and attend college full-time. Maybe it would reduce my stress if I weren't working, then I could concentrate on school and taking care of Ashlee. There's no shame in it and it would help a lot."

"You don't have to do that. I can afford to pay more."

"I know you can, Jackie, but you've done more than enough. I need to do everything I can to contribute my half of the expenses."

That night, Dana got a pen and paper and drew a line down the center of the page. She made a chart of the pluses and minuses of continuing to work and taking classes at night and of quitting work and going on welfare to complete college. Welfare won thumbs up.

The next day she contacted the Alameda County Welfare Department, got all the information she needed to apply for benefits and then made an appointment with the financial aid officer at SFSU. Within a month, she knew that she would be able to return to school full-time in the fall, not have to work, receive a full financial aid package and welfare benefits.

Since she changed her major from social work to business administration, she also met with a guidance counselor at SFSU. She wanted to ensure she had all the classes required to graduate the following spring. When he went through her transcripts, he told her, "You're actually close to being able to get a dual degree; one in social work and the other in business administration, but it will take you two years instead of one."

She was surprised; those were the two areas that she was the most interested in, but she hadn't considered a dual degree.

"You need to take an Introduction to Business Law class during the summer, but you can take that course at a local junior college, then you'll only have four semesters to go and you can graduate in two years."

"That's perfect. I want to finish college by the time my daughter begins preschool."

Dana continued to work at the travel agency and enrolled in the Introduction to Business Law Class for the 1979 summer session. Now she had more time with Ashlee.

She bought a bike with an infant's seat at a yard sale, so she and Ashlee spent late afternoons riding around Lake Merritt.

Soon Dana would be in college full-time and receiving a welfare subsidy, so she wouldn't have much money for extras. The bike ride allowed her and Ashlee to have an excursion and provided her with some much-needed exercise. Most of all she didn't have to spend any money.

One bright, sunny day she was pedaling Ashlee around Lake Merritt and the rear tire suddenly went flat. Thank goodness, she wasn't going fast. She stopped and got both of them off the bike safely. She stood there looking at the bike, but she didn't have a clue how to fix the tire.

A young African-American man was jogging nearby, saw her dilemma, and offered to help. He found a nail in the tire and suggested they take the bike to a gas station, which was close by. He steered the bike while she carried Ashlee and they briefly introduced themselves during their walk to the gas station. When he finished, she thanked him and he continued with his jog. After that, she occasionally saw him jogging and they'd say hello or wave, but she couldn't remember his name.

*1979*

# Chapter 20

Cameron worked for a prestigious international law firm, Tate, Walker and Robinson, who primarily handled contracts, liability mergers and structured financings, but he was bored. He definitely was not enjoying his work at the firm. He was doing exceptionally well and knew he would eventually be offered a partnership but that was years down the road. Sometimes he thought he would scream if he attended another meeting with billable hours as the main topic. Most of the time he would have preferred to be anywhere else other than work.

Over the last twelve years, he and Eileen had changed greatly from when they were undergrads. Back then, they were two idealistic students determined to make a difference in the black community. Both planned to complete their undergraduate degrees and go directly to graduate and law school. Afterwards, they would to return to their communities and help others. They went from being friends, who shared common interests and long-term goals, to lovers and then husband and wife when they married in 1970. He needed to believe that at some point they had been deeply in love with each other.

They were both outstanding students and as a result received excellent positions when he finished law school and Eileen completed her MBA program. Eileen was an entry-level bank officer at Wells Fargo Bank in San Francisco and he worked at a prestigious Oakland law firm. He wasn't sure when they began to rationalize that it was okay to defer their dream to help in the community. If he remembered correctly, they first justified not going back to help the black community because of the social climate in the South. Next, they would need money, and for that, they needed to work longer. Their firms emphasized volunteering in the community and they were both doing that on a limited basis so they rationalized that they were partially living up to their ideas.

He knew that snazzy new cars, expensive clothes, and corporate expense accounts constantly tempted both of them. In any case, they went from being two struggling students to living the high life.

After a while, they quit making excuses and continued earning more and more money. They were advancing up the corporate ladder, putting in long hours, and reaping the benefits with corporate bonuses, including a recent trip to Hawaii. Their parents and friends were so proud of them. Somehow, they kept deferring their original plan. There was always something, a vacation in the Caribbean, a condominium that overlooked Lake Merritt, then a home in the Oakland Hills, a Mercedes Benz for Eileen and his dream car: a Porsche. They were continuously wanting and acquiring more and more.

One day, he saw a memo circulating around the firm requesting that someone volunteer to teach an introductory business law class at night at Laney College for two semesters.

He thought this might be what he needed. It was an opportunity to do something different, something that didn't require him to think in terms of billable hours. With his schedule at the office, he rarely left for home before eight or nine at night. By teaching two nights a week, he would have to be out of the office by 6:30 p.m. in order to teach the seven o'clock course.

Before he volunteered, he met with James Avila, his mentor and boss, to discuss the assignment. James felt it would be a great opportunity since he had already proven his expertise at being an attorney. Now the partners would see him take the initiative to improve the firm's corporate image by participating in a community program. He quickly told Cameron, "Since the firm is doing other outreach programs, we should be able to get some media coverage on your assignment, maybe a spot on a local television station. This kind of visibility can also increase your billable hours and with your looks, you might become a local celebrity," he jokingly added.

The firm backed him completely even reducing his workload slightly, providing a law clerk to assist him with course development and scheduling guest speakers. Initially, the assignment was for two semesters, fall and spring. After he met with Dr. Sheldon, the dean at Laney College, they decided it would be best for him to start in the summer. The summer classes tended to be smaller, allowing him time to become comfortable with academia.

Eileen wasn't happy about him volunteering for the position. After he explained that he needed to do something different at this point in his life, she grudgingly agreed. Looking back, he realized that he and Eileen had begun drifting apart before he accepted the night school position. He was tired of the parties, social events and the cutthroat office environment. Sure, he was on track to making partner, but he had to struggle the entire time. He could honestly say it wasn't racist. It didn't matter what color you were, it was just how the game was played.

The first night he taught at Laney, students were rushing to find seats in his class. He promptly told them, "Slow down everyone, I'm not going to start for at least ten minutes."

He saw a young woman enter the classroom who looked familiar, but he couldn't recall where he knew her from. Then he remembered, he had helped her fix her bike's flat tire at Lake Merritt. He couldn't remember her name, but occasionally he saw her and her daughter biking around the lake and they waved. He thought, *Wow, small world.*

She glanced up and saw who was speaking and he acknowledged her with a nod and a smile. He took the roster and discovered that her name was Dana Adams.

He introduced himself and explained that he worked at a local law firm. "This is my first teaching assignment so hopefully we'll learn from each other." He went over his syllabus with the students, discussed his grading policy, and answered their questions. He surprised them when he gave them their assignment for the next class and dismissed them early, saying, "See you next week."

He continued to see Dana twice a week, but they rarely spoke since he usually got to class just before it started. Dana always sat in the front row and since she was an A student, they never had to meet after class.

Cameron loved teaching that summer. The majority of students were older and they worked full time jobs, so they were there because they wanted to be. The discussions were challenging and reminded him of his first year in law school. At the end of the summer session, he was looking forward to teaching the fall semester.

Joe, one of the students, told him that on Thursday evenings many of the students met after class for drinks. It gave them a chance to unwind. Surprisingly, the students asked him to join them for drinks following the last class. The exam was over and they were going out to celebrate. He initially said no, but then he thought about it. *There is no conflict of interest, each of the students is passing my class, so why not?* He and Eileen had had a disagreement that morning and he really wasn't in a hurry to go home.

He had a great time! He could not remember when he had laughed so much or felt so light hearted. Although each of the students had given him a reason why they were taking the course at the beginning of the class, he didn't know very much about them personally. He was surprised at how many had families and the sacrifices they were making in order to attend night school. Joe had a son who had leukemia so he was working to obtain his degree in order to get a job with better medical benefits.

Dana explained that she was a single parent, and needed a degree to get a better job to support her daughter. She was excited because this was her last course at Laney and she would return to college full-time to complete working on her bachelor's degree during the fall semester.

When he got home, Eileen asked why he was so late and he told her he had joined his students for drinks to celebrate the end of the class. She seemed taken aback. "Isn't that beneath you? After all, you are an attorney."

He didn't respond, but instead took a shower and went to bed. He wondered how Eileen, who had grown up dirt poor, could make such a condescending comment. It's amazing how much she's changed. *When had she become such an elitist?*

1980

# Chapter 21

Cameron enjoyed the time he spent teaching at Laney. He had even taken it upon himself to help Dr. Sheldon with a few potential legal issues, pro bono. He was surprised that he had been teaching for almost a year and it was the only thing remotely related to law that he actually enjoyed doing. Often, when he was in the office, it was the same old thing day in and day out. Yes, he was continuing to do well with billable hours, but the idea of being an attorney in a law firm for the rest of his life, even as partner, was depressing. Teaching at the junior college two nights a week provided him with an outlet from the drudgery of corporate law. He had met many students over the last year and hoped that he had made a difference in the lives of some of them.

One evening he and Dr. Sheldon, with whom he had become good friends, met for drinks and Cameron thanked him for allowing him to have such a meaningful experience.

"I rarely get that type of feedback. Generally, people in your position want to return to the corporate world as soon as possible."

"I'm sure that's true but teaching works well for me since my undergraduate minor was in education. I decided to go into law because it was prestigious and I thought I would enjoy it, but it's not all it's made up to be."

"Sounds like you're having second thoughts about your career choice."

"It's not exactly the way I planned to spend my life. It pays great money, but the costs are high too."

Later that month he received a call from Dr. Sheldon inviting him to lunch. They met at a small Chinese restaurant in downtown Oakland that served Dim Sum. After they finished eating, Dr. Sheldon quit the small talk and got down to business.

"When we talked last month I got the distinct impression that you aren't exactly happy with your career choice. Did I read that right or were you just venting?"

"No, I wasn't venting. I dread each day I go into the office."

"I received a resignation letter from Wade Hollings, the instructor who teaches the daytime Introduction to Business Law classes. He has accepted a position at the university level. If you are serious, I can offer you that position. It would require you to co-chair our Improvements Committee and it obviously won't pay the type of salary that you are accustomed to. I am impressed with your dedication to teaching and I think that you will be an asset to Laney. Why don't you take some time to think about it and get back to me in two weeks?"

Cameron was, in fact, very happy and surprised to hear what Dr. Sheldon was offering. This was his out, an opportunity to do something that helped others, not something that only made more money for the law firm. He wanted to say yes immediately, but knew he needed to take time to think about it and discuss it with Eileen.

He gave his dad a call and told him about the offer and that he wanted to say yes.

"I'm not surprised. I've heard enthusiasm in your voice each time you talk about what you're doing at the college." Then he asked, "How does Eileen feel about this?"

"She's out of town on a business trip and I'd rather talk about this face to face. You're the only one I've discussed this with."

"Good luck, whatever decision you make will be a good one."

When Eileen returned home, he waited two days before he broached the subject of a career change. When he finally decided it was time for them to discuss the issue, they were finishing dinner at home on one of the rare nights they ate together.

"We need to talk about something, Eileen."

"Sure, what."

"For a while now I've been feeling that I made the wrong career choice."

"What? Are you kidding? You mentioned that last year but I thought you were going through a phase."

"No, it's not a phase. I apologize for not telling you how serious I was, but I haven't been able to see any other options until now."

"So what's happening now?"

"You know I've been teaching a night class at Laney this past year."

"Yes, it's still surprising to me that you'd even consider teaching there; a junior college, a college for people who can't cut it at the top schools."

"Eileen, you're wrong about the school. Most of the students are people either returning to school or attempting to complete school as economically as possible. All that aside, I love teaching there, Eileen, and they've offered me an adjunct position."

She sat there staring at him. Finally, she said, "You must have lost your mind. Are you seriously considering leaving a prestigious law firm where you will eventually become partner to teach at a junior college? If I didn't know you better, I would swear that it was April 1$^{st}$ and this was your idea of an April Fool's Day joke. Do you think I plan to give up this lifestyle for you to go help some kids who can't even get into a four year college?"

Cameron shook his head and continued, "We won't have to make that many changes. You are a vice-president at the bank now, so with that increase and my reduced salary, we will still be doing well financially."

"Doing well? Well, guess what? That is not acceptable! I am not willing to settle for well. Well was a place I visited a long time ago and one I never want to visit again. I don't want well, I want excellent, the top, enough money for the lifestyle I deserve for all my hard work and struggle to get up the corporate ladder."

Cameron knew it would be difficult to persuade her to see his side. "You must have realized how dissatisfied I've been in the practice," he said. "I finally found something that I enjoy and that I have a passion for, something that allows me to give back to the community. Don't you remember what we said? We would give back to our communities when we finished college."

"Give me a break. We already send a considerable amount of money to various charities; what more do you want? Look, we made commitments when we were much younger and didn't know what the future would bring. I was brought up dirt poor

1981

# Chapter 22

Cameron and Eileen had been separated for over a year and were no closer to reconciliation than they had been when he moved out. They had begun counseling shortly after he accepted the position at Laney, but it had not gone very well. The sessions generally ended in a heated debate or with one of them shutting down and saying nothing. He knew that he needed to face the fact that they would eventually be in divorce court. He was surprised that Eileen had not filed for divorce again by now. He felt the only thing holding her back was that she knew that her current salary was considerably higher than his. Under California law, she could wind up paying him alimony and there was no way in hell she'd do that.

For him, the last year had been incredible; he was actually busier than he had been at the law firm, something he never thought possible. The difference was he enjoyed, no, loved, what he was doing as adjunct professor at Laney. He finally had work that was meaningful where he could see changes that were important to him. He was also working on his PhD in

Education and that took a great deal of his time, but, again, he thoroughly enjoyed it. He was thankful that he and Eileen had saved a considerable amount of money. Fortunately, they had more than enough in savings to pay for the courses needed to attain his doctorate.

In addition to teaching, he was actively involved in the college's Improvement Committee. Dr. Sheldon, Laney's President, was very persuasive and had secured a local marketing firm to work with the college pro bono. Their objective was to determine why enrollment was decreasing and to develop strategies to increase student enrollment. Cameron was asked to chair the committee.

One of the recommendations was to conduct focus groups with recent Laney graduates and with students who had attended, but did not graduate. During the focus groups, Cameron sat in an adjoining room, with other members of the committee, behind a glass window observing the participants. They randomly selected focus group participants who received a check for their participation.

The final focus group was held in late January and Cameron was surprised to see Dana was a participant. He hadn't seen her in over a year and she had changed a great deal. The woman he was looking at now had matured. He had always seen her in casual clothes; bike riding with her daughter around the lake, or in night classes in jeans or sweats. The woman on the other side of the window was dressed in a flattering black pants suit with an off-white blouse and pearls and matching earrings. With her short haircut, much shorter than when he last saw her, she was stunning.

During the focus group, the moderator asked a series of questions intended to get a sense of what the participants' experience at Laney was like. Dana was thoughtful before she described how Laney had been one of the best opportunities for her. It allowed her to finish her associate's degree at a lower cost and be closer to home.

An hour after the session ended, as he was exiting the administrative building, he ran into Dana and another woman outside. As he walked toward them, Dana looked up and was surprised to see him.

"Mr. Mitchell! Wow! Good to see you. I didn't know you were still teaching here. This is my friend, Wanda Elliot."

"First of all, you can call me Cameron. Glad to meet you, Wanda."

"Are you still teaching Intro to Business Law?"

"Yes, I am, but now I'm on staff at Laney. I left the law firm over a year ago."

"Really," Dana said. "What a surprise."

They talked for a while and the next thing he knew, Wanda was leaving saying, "I've got to get out of here. I told my cousin that I'd pick up the kids by seven and its six forty-five." They continued talking and Dana told him she was going to a coffee shop and invited him to join her.

Since he and Eileen had separated and he left the law firm, he hadn't been out much at night. He usually went to the gym after work and then headed home to study. When they got to the coffee shop, he was surprised at how crowded it was. After they got their coffee, he and Dana began talking. Dana brought him up to date on some of the students who had been in the class. She also told him she had one more semester to complete at San Francisco State and she would have her bachelor's degree.

She continued, "I had an interview at a nonprofit organization earlier today. I don't expect to get the position since I won't finish college until next semester, but it was good getting the interview experience."

When he looked at his watch, it was 8:00 p.m.

"Don't you have to get home to that beautiful daughter of yours?"

"No, I'm not in a big hurry. Ashlee is in Lake Tahoe with her godmother this week. As a matter of fact, she's been gone for two days and as usual I'm missing her." Then she apologized, "Sorry I'm holding you up."

"No you're not; I'd only be at home studying. I'm working on my doctorate, but I'm current on my assignments right now."

"That sounds interesting."

Cameron was usually quiet, but he found himself telling Dana that he and his wife separated last year but were in marriage counseling.

Dana listened as he talked.

"We thought the separation would be good for both of us and the marriage counseling would help us resolve our issues, but it seems as if we are getting further apart. As I sit across from her during the weekly sessions, it's like I am talking to a total stranger." Then he stopped, "Sorry, I shouldn't be bothering you with all of this."

"No problem, I can definitely identify with being separated. I hope everything works out for both of you."

The coffee crew began cleaning up and Dana and Cameron were the last two customers. When they got up to leave, Cameron knew he didn't want the evening to end so he asked, "Would you like to get something to eat? I'm not sure about you, but I'm starving."

"Sure."

"Let's go down to Jack London Square. We can walk there from here."

"Perfect, I haven't been there in a while," Dana said. What Cameron didn't say was that restaurants were out of his budget these days, *but so what*, he thought, *I need an evening out*.

They went to a small restaurant overlooking the water, where they enjoyed a delicious seafood meal and headed to the bar area to listen to music after dinner. The next thing they knew, it was almost 11:00 p.m. and both of them said they had to get home so they could get some sleep.

As they walked to Dana's car, they talked about how much they enjoyed the evening. As Dana was getting in her car, he asked her if she would like to go to San Francisco the next weekend.

"I had a great time tonight, but you're married, Cameron. A day in the city isn't something I'd like to do with a married man."

"Sorry, I understand, but I wasn't really thinking of it as a date. I was comfortable with you, and because we had a lot of things in common, I thought it'd be fun to go to the city."

Dana relented and said, "Okay, since you put it like that and it's not a date." She quickly gave him her phone number before she left.

"Great, I'll call you on Friday to firm up where we can meet."

During the week, Cameron thought about the time he'd spent with Dana and considered calling her, but after all he was married and Saturday would only be hanging out with a friend.

Cameron picked up Dana at her apartment and he met her best friend, Jackie, who was watching Ashlee for the day.

They took the Bay Area Rapid Transit (BART) to the city and rode cable cars, walked around Fisherman's Wharf and Japan Town, and finally ended the evening in China Town for dinner. He could not remember having so much fun in a long time. They both had forgotten how cold San Francisco was at night and hadn't dressed properly. They found themselves huddling up to each other on the way back on BART and making plans to go to Napa, to wine country, next month where it would be much warmer.

They didn't consider themselves dating. They justified it that way, since Dana was dating another person and Cameron was still attending marriage counseling. At first, they were "hang out" friends, but soon they were doing more and more things together. He knew that it was past the friendship stage for him but he kept his feelings to himself. During one of their conversations, Dana informed him that she had no interest in a relationship with a married man, even one legally separated.

One Friday, Cameron received a call from a friend who asked if he wanted two free tickets to a Patty LaBelle concert that night. He had an emergency and couldn't attend. Cameron said definitely and called Dana to see if she wanted to go. She quickly agreed and he told her what time he'd pick her up. When Cameron arrived, Dana was wearing a black leather blazer with dark slacks and a multi-colored blouse and she looked fantastic.

"Where's your daughter?"

"With Jackie, she's taking her to Tahoe again for the weekend. A friend of Jackie's has a cabin up there and they go up on weekends so the kids can play in the snow."

They both enjoyed the performance. Cameron had seen Patty perform in other venues, but she was always at her best in San Francisco where she had a strong following from the gay community that turned out en masse to see her.

When they left the concert, he suggested stopping for drinks when they got back to Oakland. When they reached downtown Oakland, it began pouring down rain. Cameron was driving down Broadway when a driver cut in front of him and stopped suddenly. He quickly slammed on the brakes to avoid hitting the vehicle. He hit a wet, slick spot and the car spun out of control causing it to cross the centerline. Dana screamed as Cameron attempted to gain control, barely missing an oncoming vehicle. He finally regained control and pulled over; shaken.

"Wow, that was scary," said Dana.

He said, "I can't believe that. I didn't think I was going to get out of that spin without us being in a serious accident."

"Let's skip drinks. I'm a little shook up," said Dana.

When they arrived at her apartment, Dana invited Cameron up saying, "I think I have a bottle of wine in the fridge."

While she was getting the wine, Cameron walked over to the patio door and looked out. "Wow, I didn't realize what an awesome view you have."

"Yeah, that's definitely what sold me on this apartment, plus it was affordable. Grab a couple of pillows off the couch and we can sit by the window, but I have to warn you it gets a little chilly there sometimes." She dimmed the apartment lights so the view of Lake Merritt was even more spectacular.

After she poured them each a glass of wine, she joined Cameron and they sat on the pillows sipping wine and talking. Dana shivered and Cameron instinctively reached out and held her and she lay in his arms. Somehow, it felt right, she turned her face toward him, and their lips met. He could taste the wine on her lips, and what started as a gentle kiss, got deeper and deeper. He could feel himself getting an erection and tried to control his body. He pulled back; one of the hardest things he'd ever done.

During the last months of their marriage, Eileen had sex only as a duty. She had changed her hairstyle to an expensive weave and she didn't want to do anything to mess it up, especially sex. He had a few casual sexual encounters immediately after the separation, which meant nothing. He hadn't made love in months now.

Dana reached up and put her hand behind his head, gently nudging his mouth back to hers. The next thing he knew, he was unbuttoning her blouse. He stopped before removing her blouse and asked her, "Are you sure?"

"I'm definitely sure, I've wanted this for longer than you can imagine."

From then on he wasn't sure of who did what. In what seemed like hours later, he was holding Dana in his arms. They had never left the living room floor. He had never made love like this before; never with this kind of mental and physical intensity.

Later they got up and went into Dana's bedroom. In the back of his mind, he was hoping and praying that Dana wouldn't look at him later and say she regretted what happened. She must have read his mind because the next thing he heard her say was, "I will never regret this."

He pulled her closer to him, kissed the top of her head, her eyes, her mouth, her neck, her breasts and they began making love over and over, again and again until they finally drifted off to sleep.

# Chapter 23

Dana was originally scheduled to graduate in May, 1981, but when her advisor reviewed her final transcripts, he realized that two courses from her first year in college would not be accepted. As a result, she would need to take the courses during the summer and graduate in August. She was disappointed, but it was a short period, and then it would all be over. Her parents planned to take Ashlee home to Ohio with them for the summer immediately after Dana graduated; instead, Dana took her to Ohio over the Memorial Day weekend.

Jackie had moved to a smaller apartment in the same building in January so that Dana and Ashlee could have more space. When Dana returned from Ohio, she and Cameron became inseparable. With Ashlee being away, they spent most nights at her apartment. She studied for her last two courses and Cameron worked on one of his many job or school related projects. They spent time talking, listening to music, and making love. They carefully avoided talking about the fact that they were in a relationship. It was easier for them to ignore the fact that Cameron was still married. With Ashlee coming home in two weeks and Dana graduating the weekend after that, they knew their situation would be short-lived. For now, they pretended everything was okay.

The next two weeks flew by and she was so excited that after all these years, she was finally completing college. It had been a long road, but today that journey was over. Dana was about to graduate with a joint degree, one in Business Administration and the other in Social Work.

As she marched with her classmates into the San Francisco State University auditorium, she was proud of herself. Since it was an August graduation, there weren't as many graduates as usual. She was able to see Ashlee sitting with Jackie and waving at her when her class entered. She hoped that Ashlee would remember this day when it was time for her to go to college and not take detours like her mom had taken.

Dana was sorry her parent's could not attend. A week prior to graduation, her dad sustained a back injury while loading a heavy box at work. He was hospitalized but released earlier this week. He required around the clock care so her mom and brothers were home helping him.

She wondered what she was going to do now that she had completed college. She had applied for a number of jobs in the Bay Area and in Ohio but hadn't heard anything yet. Finally, she decided to enjoy the day and allow the future to take care of itself. Then she heard the dean calling her name and she was walking across the stage; accepting her diplomas, she thought, *this is real.*

Cameron attended the ceremony and afterwards they all went out for a late lunch. As they were leaving the restaurant Cameron said, "I have a surprise for you. I'm taking you to Monterey for your graduation gift."

She had lived in the Bay Area for years, and visited many areas, like Santa Cruz, and Lake Tahoe, but never Monterey. He knew it was a place she'd enjoy visiting.

"I can't leave."

Jackie said, "Yes you can, I took off from work for the next few days to take care of Ashlee, you deserve this."

She was so happy and surprised that Jackie and Cameron had planned such a great graduation gift.

"What about my clothes?" Cameron opened his car trunk and showed her the suitcase that Jackie had packed. She finally got the idea when Ashlee told her, "Bye, Mommy, I'm going home with Auntie Jackie."

She hugged Jackie and Ashlee and they left immediately.

They drove down Highway 101 stopping at a roadside vendor to purchase fruit. Cameron continued driving and connected to Highway 1, which allowed them to enjoy the scenic route to Monterey with the Pacific Ocean shimmering in the distance.

Cameron had selected a five star hotel. He had recently completed a consulting job and was using part of that money for Dana's graduation gift. From the outside, it was a quaint unassuming hotel, but from the time they arrived the level of service was impeccable, from the valet parking service to the ease of check in.

When the bellman opened the door to their room, it was majestic; tastefully decorated in soft greens, beiges and hints of peach. There was a spectacular view of the Pacific, which they could see through the partially opened patio drapes. There was also a fruit basket, a bottle of champagne, and cheese and crackers in the suite.

Although it was August, Monterey was still seasonably cold. They walked through the city in wool jackets, holding hands and discovering shops. Finally, they ended up walking along the water, where they sat on a large rock, and talked. Dana and Cameron were enjoying the trip and it allowed them time to discuss their relationship and his marital status, a subject that they had been avoiding.

"I've been feeling a little guilty about this, Cameron. We've come a long way from being 'hang out' buddies."

"I agree," Cameron had to admit. "This isn't what I planned and I've got to do something about it. I have another counseling session in two weeks, and I'm going to tell Eileen I want a divorce."

"I don't want you to do that because of me."

He smiled and said, "No, it's not about you, although you are very important and I care about you. My marriage was in the pits long before I met you. Eileen and I are in two different places and it doesn't seem that we can connect any longer. Spending this summer with you has been great; it has been a very different world for me, very relaxed, no pretense. More importantly, it showed me the kind of world I want at this point in my life."

Dana didn't respond because she was unsure of her feelings.

They spent the rest of the weekend exploring the city, the surrounding areas, and trying various restaurants. On the drive back to Oakland, reality began to set in and she knew she had a great deal of things to do the following week, including submitting more job applications. They talked briefly about job possibilities and she told Cameron that she was applying for positions in both fields in Ohio and the Bay Area.

He was surprised, "I didn't realize you were considering returning to Ohio."

She told him that she had been thinking about going home for a while since she was so far away from her family and she missed them. She added that she had been very fortunate to have Jackie as her support system, but that would probably change.

"I think Jackie wants to move back to the East Coast so she can be closer to her grandmother, although she won't come right out and say it," she said. "With that possibility, Ohio is definitely up for consideration."

Although he was disturbed at the idea of Dana leaving, he said, "Right, I can see why returning to Ohio would be an option."

When she got home, Dana told Jackie about Cameron's plan to ask his wife for a divorce.

"How do you feel about that?"

"I really don't know. I really enjoy being with him, but we've only been going out a few months and most of that time we were friends. Things have changed since we became intimately involved. Right now all I know is I care a lot about him. I want to be sure that if he gets a divorce, it's not because of me."

They were both very busy after their trip to Monterey so they didn't see each other the week after they returned. They had dinner the second week and Cameron told her he was meeting with the marriage counselor and Eileen the following Wednesday.

She told him about her week and that she had heard from two employers about jobs, one in San Francisco and one in Cincinnati. The one in San Francisco was an entry-level accountant position and the one in Cincinnati was an assistant manager in a large nursing home.

"Which one do you want?"

"I'd prefer the job in Cincinnati because it would allow me to use both my degrees. I would be working with seniors and their families for placement and working accounts receivables in the Accounting Department."

"It sounds interesting." Then he added, "Is there any way I could persuade you to consider staying out here?"

She looked directly at him and said, "Maybe."

He leaned across the table, kissed her and said, "Let's get out of here."

They spent the night at his apartment and when she awoke the next morning, Cameron was in the kitchen cooking breakfast. She brushed her teeth and went into the small kitchen area, where he had set the table. He said, "I thought I should start working right away on convincing you to stay."

# Chapter 24

The following Monday, Cameron received a surprise call from Eileen. She asked him to meet her for a special session that afternoon in the office of Lillian Jackson, their marriage counselor.

"What's this about, Eileen? You know I don't think counseling is changing anything. I think it's time that we both accept the fact that our marriage is over and file for divorce."

"Cameron, please do me this favor and come to the session."

He reluctantly agreed and arrived on time at Dr. Johnson's office.

Before he could speak, Lillian said that Eileen had something to share with him. Eileen was sitting in a beige oversized leather chair to his immediate right. He noticed that she was red eyed and had a handkerchief in her hand that she kept balling up.

She turned to face him and said, in a voice so low he could barely hear her, "I have Multiple Sclerosis."

Initially, he didn't think he'd heard her right.

She continued, "For the last few months, I've been struggling with fatigue, dizziness, tingling in my hands…I even fainted at the office one day. My doctor referred me to a neurologist and the results came back yesterday."

Lillian got up from her seat and said, "I think I need to leave you two alone, if you want me, I'll be in the adjoining conference room."

They sat there in silence for a few minutes and Cameron asked, "What's going to happen next?"

Eileen told him that she had another appointment with the neurologist, Dr. Berg, in the morning and Cameron told her he would go with her.

They left the marriage counselor's office and Cameron followed Eileen home that night, entering their house for the first time in months. They sat in the living room and talked and she tried to tell him what the doctor told her. She admitted that she was so shocked that she probably didn't get it right. Since it was late, Cameron decided to stay over, went to the guestroom, and grabbed a pair of pajama bottoms that he had left there.

Cameron didn't get much sleep that night. He tossed and turned, playing devil's advocate, *what if the diagnosis is wrong, let's get the top expert in this field to review the medical information. What if this isn't a serious case of MS?*

The next morning they arrived at Dr. Berg's office promptly at 9:00 a.m. Eileen introduced them, and he quickly began by saying, "I was hoping for better news, but I've consulted another neurologist in my practice who concurs with my diagnosis. There's actually no test that can be performed to diagnose MS so we reached our diagnosis based on the series of problems you've been experiencing."

beginning of their fiscal year. She called them promptly and accepted the position, and then she called her parents and Jackie to tell them the news.

She waited to tell Cameron that she had accepted the position in Ohio until everything was in motion and there was virtually no way to change her plans. She invited him over for dinner and cooked a steak, baked potato, broccoli and a salad. After dinner, they sat on pillows in the living room looking out the patio window at the Lake Merritt area. Then she told him. Cameron was stunned.

"Dana, why did you wait to tell me? Based on what you're saying, you'll be leaving at the end of the week, three days from now."

"I know, but you've been busy with Eileen and I had a lot of things to do in a short amount of time. I didn't want to take you away from what you needed to do. I wanted to tell you when we were face to face."

"What am I going to do without you?"

"You're going to continue doing what you're doing now, being supportive of your wife."

They both sat there not saying anything, and finally Cameron spoke. "I've been deluding myself for the last few weeks, knowing that I wouldn't be able to get a divorce now, not with Eileen having MS. Somehow I kept thinking that eventually this would work out. You're doing the right thing, going forward with your life. If you stayed here, I cannot promise you that I wouldn't attempt to continue seeing you and that wouldn't be fair to you. You deserve much better than that."

"I am going to miss you so much."

"I need to tell you one thing, Dana. Even though it's been a short time, you have made my life much better than it's been in a very long time."

Cameron took her in his arms and held her closely. They sat on the floor, looking at the view, each in their own thoughts and finally they made love for the last time. They spent the night on the living room floor, grabbing some throws from a basket next to the couch.

In the morning, Cameron asked her, "Will I see you before you leave?"

"No, I booked my schedule so I don't have any free time from now until we leave. The movers will be here tomorrow and Jackie and I will be working nonstop today getting ready for them. Are you okay?"

"I'm okay right now," he said. "I have the touch and feel of you on my body. I don't know how I will be next week...next month."

He kissed her and left. Dana closed the door, sat on the couch crying until Jackie rang her doorbell.

*Chapter 26*

With Dana and Ashlee moving, Jackie decided it was time for her to make some decisions about her future. She passed the California Bar Exam on her first attempt in 1979. She was proud of herself because California had one of the most difficult bar exams in the country. As she looked back now, she realized she hadn't done very much since then.

Her divorce became final in March 1979, and at that time, she was still having difficulty accepting how her marriage ended. She received a generous settlement and alimony from Gary with the stipulation that she not disclose the reason for the divorce. With the settlement, she really didn't need a position that paid a great deal of money. She accepted the first job offered to her at Baldwin & Baldwin Attorneys at Law. It was a small Oakland family owned firm, which didn't have much growth potential. It allowed her to have a flexible schedule and help with Ashlee while Dana completed her undergraduate degree. She would not have changed that for anything.

Now she wondered, *what happened to the ambitious young lady who in high school planned to be such a success? The one who finished law school at Columbia in the top 5% of her class with lofty aspirations to make partner in a prestigious law firm? Had she allowed her dreams to die?* She had used the excuse that she was helping Dana with Ashlee, but that wasn't the reason and she knew it. In reality, she had been having her own private pity party. She had become complacent. As she thought about the last three years, she realized that she allowed her divorce from Gary to hinder her career, and had no one to blame but herself. She was no longer the person who always had a goal, who wanted to be successful. The realization came over her like a light in a dark room; she had been drifting the entire three years she lived in the Bay Area.

The last three years allowed her to heal after her disastrous marriage, but now it was time for her to move forward and get her career back on track. She had nursed her personal pain for far too long, and as a result, her career stagnated.

She decided that now was the perfect time for her to go ahead with her plan to leave. She had made friends and had an active social life in Oakland, but it wasn't enough to keep her in the area. She had always known that although she loved the Bay Area, she would not stay permanently.

She knew that she didn't want to move back to Virginia, but she thought it would be nice to move closer to Gran, where she could get a flight home in a couple of hours. She investigated various areas, but Washington was the most promising and she loved the political energy in that area. She had watched how her Aunt Mildred had progressed there since she left Virginia. She didn't even have a high school diploma, but managed to obtain her GED and then go on to college. Now she was in a high government position. When Jackie told her she was considering a move to the city, she was ecstatic.

Jackie told a co-worker that she was considering moving back East and she referred her to Nadine Pierce, an employment recruiter she knew in the DC area. Jackie had spoken to Nadine last week, and mailed her resume with recent job performance reviews. She expected to hear from her soon. She hadn't told Dana yet, but she planned to tell her as soon as she was settled in and they could have a long conversation.

# Chapter 27

Dana was extremely busy when she returned to Cincinnati. She quickly realized that it was going to take a great deal of work to get ready for her new job in such a short time frame. First, she had to enroll Ashlee in a day care program. Her mom located two very good schools for her to consider. She needed to interview them, and have Ashlee go with her to see which one was the best fit for her personality. She had not considered that she would need to organize the bedrooms that she and Ashlee would occupy. Her mom had been so busy helping her dad, who was still recovering from his on-the-job accident, that she hadn't had time to clean out the rooms.

There was one good thing about being so busy; she didn't think about Cameron until she was in bed at night, bone tired. She had a picture of the two of them next to her bed that she looked at each night. She had even reached for the phone to call him on numerous occasions. One time she actually dialed his work number, but hung up before the call went through. She wanted to hear his voice one more time. Finally, she decided to quit putting herself through unnecessary pain. She put the picture at the back of her high school photo album, a place where she would not be looking in any time soon.

Tonight after she got Ashlee into bed and read her a story, she gave Jackie a call. Right away Jackie told Dana that she had contacted a recruiter regarding a position in DC.

"That's exciting, but when did you decide?"

"I've known for a while that I wanted to get closer to Gran, so when you decided to move to Ohio, I knew it was time for me to move too."

"I'm so sorry I've been holding you up."

"No, you didn't hold me up. I really wasn't ready to leave until now."

"Have you heard anything from the recruiter?"

"Yes, I heard from her earlier this week and right now things aren't looking very good. It seems that I don't have enough specialized experience. She said that even though I have an impressive resume, the main problem is that I don't have an area of expertise."

"But you've handled all types of cases."

"You're right, but now I'm trying to get into one of the top firms on the east coast and the rules are different. Baldwin & Baldwin is so small that each attorney is expected to handle any case they are assigned. As a result, I've handled everything from divorces to adoptions and even a few criminal cases."

"I know you, so I know you have a plan. So spill it out."

Jackie laughed. "Yeah, you know me. I do have a plan. Based on what the recruiter told me, many firms in the area are looking for attorneys with expertise in establishing trusts and knowledge of the tax ramifications."

"Exactly what is a trust?"

"There are various types of trusts, the ones most people hear about are for wealthy individuals; people with huge estates like the Kennedys. With a trust, a person can pass their assets to whomever they want without having to go through the courts or probate. Because trusts are private, there is no public record. Trusts are an area that I enjoyed studying in law school, but have only worked on a limited basis since I joined Baldwin & Baldwin."

"Recently our firm won a class action lawsuit. We represented over 50 clients who were exposed to a dangerous chemical at their company, resulting in major medical problems. Since it was a prominent company in the Bay Area, initially the litigants had difficulty getting adequate counsel. The large firms did not want to litigate against the corporation, but Baldwin & Baldwin accepted the case shortly after I was hired."

"I remember that case. It was in all the papers and you even told me about it."

"Right, well, normally these types of cases go on and on with one continuance after another. Fortunately, for our firm, one of the company's owners jilted his girlfriend who was also his secretary. She provided us with information in the form of letters and memos showing that the manufacturer warned the company of the risks associated with using the chemicals. The company decided to ignore them. When we presented the information to the company and its attorneys they decided to settle out of court with the litigants. Each litigant will receive an average of $1.5 million and the company is responsible for all the litigants' legal costs."

"What are the litigants going to do now? It sounds like they won't be able to work again. Although it's a substantial sum of money they could go through it quickly if they're not careful."

"Right, and that's where the trusts come in. Walter Baldwin, the senior partner, recently broached the subject of our firm expanding into the trust field during our staff meeting. He acknowledged that this was the biggest case that the firm had ever won but he was concerned that the litigants might mismanage the funds. That would be detrimental for many of them since they will be unable to work and they need the money for their livelihood. He wanted to ensure that their future was secure. He stressed that by establishing trusts; there would be a safeguard for the litigant's monies since many have small children."

"Going into the area of trusts would bring additional revenues to Baldwin & Baldwin. The firm had done a few trusts but larger firms usually handle this area. Since I want to expand my resume, I volunteered to spearhead the effort. Walter was so happy that he promptly committed to providing me with immediate training. As a result, I will be attending an intense two-week training course on trusts at Georgetown University beginning next week."

"Wow, I'm so happy for you."

"I'm looking forward to the training and to the trip. I plan to take my vacation while I'm back east, go to Virginia, and spend some time with Gran. Hopefully, with the training and starting up the trust division, it will eventually get me the position I want."

It was almost midnight and Dana was yawning. Before they hung-up, they agreed that Jackie would call the following week.

*1982*

# Chapter 28

Jackie was devastated it had been over six months and Nadine was unable to find her a position. She hadn't contemplated not being able to get a job. She knew that it would probably be an entry-level position and she was okay with that. Not having any offers in six months was totally unexpected. She had completed the training course on trusts and the start-up of the trust division at Baldwin & Baldwin was going relatively smooth. She thought that with the added training and experience on her revised resume, she'd definitely be offered a position. Right now, she was at a low and she decided that she would take the next twenty-four hours to feel sorry for herself. She could cry, moan or groan during that period, but when it was over, she needed to get busy and decide exactly what she wanted and what to do to get it.

Exactly twenty-four hours later, she began working on her strategic plan. She had turned twenty-nine so she decided to set her goal to become a partner in a prestigious Washington, DC firm by the time she was 45. She was enjoying working the trust side of law, but she wanted to ensure that it was a lucrative field, one in which she would ultimately make partner.

She had been working on her career goals by herself and now she needed a sounding board, someone in her field with whom she could discuss her plan. She decided to contact Matt Rawlins, one of her old law professors at Columbia. Matt had been one of her favorite instructors and she maintained contact with him. They had a very good relationship. She knew he would be candid and provide her with honest feedback. Matt had been with a large New York law firm and left it for academia, but he maintained contacts in the legal community. She reached him as he was returning to his office from teaching his morning classes. They talked for a while, catching up on various people they both kept in contact with.

Jackie finally said, "I need your opinion."

"Sure, what's up?"

Jackie explained how she had spent the last six months looking for a position in the DC area and received no job offers. She shared with him the feedback she received from Nadine. She told him that she was heading up the newly formed trust area for her firm and thought that when she included that experience on her resume it would open some doors, but it had not.

"You're on the right track, but be sure to also include the Estate and Gift (E&G) side of the law." He recommended that she take as many continuing professional education (CPE) courses in E&G and trust law as possible and consider getting her MBA with an emphasis in taxation. "What you really want to do is to become an expert in these areas, with thorough knowledge of the law, its tax consequences, and all its intricacies. As soon as you have that knowledge under your belt, try to instruct at a technical session in your area. That way your name will be out there."

Jackie absorbed all he said, "Thank you so much."

"No problem, you were always a very good student, sounds like you got a little side tracked. By the way, I have a good friend, Franklin Kingsford, who can probably provide some additional information. He's also a Columbia graduate and partner at one of the biggest firms in Washington and he specializes in E&G. I'll give you his information. I owe him a call anyway, so I'll contact him when I hang up and tell him to expect a call from you."

When they ended the conversation, Jackie felt relieved; she was on the right path. She did some additional research on the E&G side of the law and contacted Franklin Kingsford the next day.

Franklin was easy to talk to and reinforced what Matt had told her. At the end of their conversation, he said, "If you're ever in the area, please give me a call."

Jackie spent the rest of '82 studying E&G law and building up her firm's new trust department. She was enjoying her work, and for the first time in her career, she was putting in extremely long hours. She didn't mind because it was all part of her strategic plan. In addition, she and Matt had begun talking on a monthly basis and he quickly became her mentor.

Franklin mentioned to Matt that he needed a female attorney to participate on an E&G panel discussion at George Washington University, and Matt recommended her. When she contacted Franklin to confirm the engagement, he suggested that they have lunch while she was in the city.

They met the day before the panel discussion was scheduled to begin at Sequoias' Restaurant. When she reached the restaurant, Franklin was arriving and the hostess escorted them to one of their best tables, overlooking the Potomac River.

They made small talk over lunch and she learned that they shared some common themes in their lives. He was from Wisconsin and had grown up as he said, "Poorer than dirt." Thanks to a high school teacher who took a special interest in him, he learned about Columbia. The teacher continued mentoring him during college and was instrumental in his applying to Columbia. Ultimately, he was accepted and his life changed dramatically after that.

After they finished eating, he asked if she wanted dessert, and she said, "No, but a cup of coffee would be great."

While they waited, he began giving her the history of Stevens, Laramie, Zuckerman, and Wilson, Attorneys at Law, and what they were currently doing in the Estate and Gift area. "As you know, E&G clients expect their attorneys to be current on all aspects of the law to ensure that their assets are safeguarded. Lately, we haven't been able to attract attorneys who are as proficient in this aspect of the law as we would like. I was impressed when you first contacted me and based on our conversation today, I can see that you have been working hard."

What Jackie didn't tell him was that she had researched the top ten firms in the area, and his firm was a definite number one. In addition to being number one, they had the best track record for hiring females and minorities, which gave them an edge in her mind.

Then Franklin surprised her. "If you continue to work diligently in the Trust Department at your current firm, stay on the path you're on now, I will personally make you an offer to join our firm. You need to understand that it will probably take at least two years, and you will be working extremely hard the entire time."

She was shocked, having had no idea there would be a potential job offer. She thanked him and told that she would keep in contact with him.

The following evening, she met Aunt Mildred for dinner and told her about the surprise turn of events during lunch with Franklin. Her aunt told her she had heard about the close connections and support systems that Ivy League school graduates maintained. She was impressed, "They definitely look out for their own."

"I'm thinking about purchasing some property here now. I can use it as an investment until I move here in a few years. I am so excited about living in the nation's capital and I can't wait to move."

"That's a good idea. There are many great areas here, but I think you might like the Capitol Hill section; it is expensive, but convenient to everything in the district. A friend of mine, Theresa Nelson, is a real estate agent. If you'd like, I can contact her and arrange for you to look at some properties before you leave."

"Thanks that would be great."

When she returned to her hotel later that evening, she couldn't believe what had transpired in the last two days. She had a potential job offer and an opportunity to purchase investment property. She had wisely invested the settlement money from her divorce. With her excellent credit, she knew she could afford property in the area.

She had scheduled two days to spend with Aunt Mildred following the panel discussion so it was a perfect time for her to look at real estate. Her aunt and Theresa picked her up when the conference ended and they immediately began looking at properties.

Although they looked in numerous areas that day, after seeing the Capitol Hill section, Jackie knew that it was the one for her. Her only concern was whether she would be able to rent the property until she moved. Theresa put her in touch with a leasing company that assured her that real estate in the area was extremely easy to rent.

The following day, they found a townhouse that was under renovation. When she walked through the unit, she knew it was the one for her. She had been considering purchasing a house for a while so she had a checklist of what she wanted in a home. It was a two-bedroom townhouse. It was an end unit, so she would get direct sunlight. There was a half bath on the first floor and a fireplace in the living room. The master bedroom was spacious and located on the second floor, with a small adjoining study and excellent closet space. The backyard had a small courtyard and it was less than a ten minute walk to METRO. The townhouse wouldn't be completed for four months, but Jackie put an offer on it that day.

When she returned to Oakland, she called Dana and told her everything that had happened. As usual, Dana was two hundred percent in her corner. Dana teased her, "I know you'll be the first African-American female Supreme Court Justice, but take some time for some fun too. Maybe do a little bit of dating."

She responded defensively, "I do date occasionally." What she didn't tell her was that her relationships never lasted long.

The following week her offer was accepted and Aunt Mildred promised to keep an eye on the construction work, "To make sure they aren't doing shoddy work." Four months later, the renovations to the townhouse were complete and she immediately leased it out.

1983

# Chapter 29

Before Dana knew it, two years had passed. She and Ashlee still stayed with her parents and she continued to work at the nursing home. She had saved a considerable amount of money, which she planned to use to purchase a home in another year. She was involved with Ashlee in various activities and routinely volunteered at her church and in her community. She had made a few friends through work and church and she enjoyed doing social activities with them. Overall, she was content.

She met Bob Richardson shortly after she returned to Ohio. Her mom told her about a man who was helping senior citizens in the community with getting reasonably priced home repairs, like having their homes winterized. He had been raised two blocks from where they lived, but he was ten years older than she was and she didn't know him.

One day she was outside in the front yard with her mom planting flowers and Bob stopped by to see if the contractor had completed placing handrails on the back stairs. Her mom introduced them and Dana commented on the changes she saw in the neighborhood. He had initiated a neighborhood watch, when negative elements moved in the area, and now the community was returning to the one she remembered. She told him that it was nice to return home and feel that she was in a safe environment.

They continued to talk about people they both knew from the neighborhood. Bob helped finish planting the flowers, then her Mom asked him to join them for dinner. Dinner was enjoyable and Dana found out a great deal about Bob. He joined the Army immediately after high school and had traveled around the world during his career. He decided to return to Cincinnati after retiring from the military since his grandparents, who raised him, left their home to him when they died. Now he was a student at the University of Cincinnati where he was working on his Masters in Public Administration. He was currently working part-time for the City of Cincinnati and devoting his spare time to helping seniors.

After Bob left, her mom told her that he was divorced, however, she wasn't interested. She acknowledged that he was an attractive and articulate man, but after Michael and then Cameron, she really wasn't interested in dating. Thanks to Ashlee, that soon changed.

Somehow, Bob seemed to be around more, dropping by to check on her parents and occasionally having dinner with them. For Ashlee's fifth birthday, Jackie sent money to buy her a bike. Bob put the training wheels on for her and taught her how to ride. He didn't have children, but he loved doing things with kids. When he finished teaching Ashlee to ride her bike, he asked Dana if she would like to go to a movie with him that evening. She hadn't dated anyone since she returned to Ohio so she promptly said, "No thanks, I've got to get Ashlee ready for bed."

Ashlee quickly piped in, "I'm five now, I can get myself ready for bed."

Dana's mom was on the porch and overheard the conversation and smiled before she said, "I'll help you, Ashlee." The next thing Dana knew she had agreed she'd be ready at 7:00 p.m.

They enjoyed the movie and stopped at LaRosa's for some of Cincinnati's finest pizza after the movie. She and Bob were working on two committees in the neighborhood, so she knew a little about his personal life. His grandmother had raised him after his mom died when he was young. That night as they enjoyed pizza, he filled in the missing details.

He told her that he'd married a young lady while he was in the military, but the marriage hadn't worked out. Since his grandparents were such positive role models, he decided to return to the area when he retired and work to improve the lives of senior citizens in the community.

They had a nice evening and agreed to go to Winton Woods the next weekend and take Ashlee with them so she could ride her bike.

Soon they were officially dating and it felt good. Dana didn't have the same kind of feelings for Bob that she had for Michael or Cameron, which she was glad about. She had her heart broken in both instances and this time she wasn't looking for that kind of passion or drama in a relationship. She wanted a stable partnership, one that would build slowly. She enjoyed being with Bob and Ashlee loved them being together.

Dana told Jackie all about Bob and she was happy for her. They continued to talk weekly, but not as long since Jackie was working long hours at the firm. In a period of less than two years, she was already building a reputation as an expert in the trust field. When she visited Cincinnati on her way to a trust conference in Chicago, she had an opportunity to meet

Bob and she was impressed. Since they shared being raised by grandparents, they had an immediate connection, quickly becoming friends.

Dana was enjoying her life, but she couldn't get rid of the migraine headaches, which were becoming more frequent. She had gone to two doctors, but they told her exactly what the doctor in California said, that the migraines were due to stress. One physician explained that stress can manifest even in positive situations. She had migraines so frequently that even Ashlee knew what to do: close the door, turn out the lights and let her mom sleep. Sleeping seemed to be the only thing that gave her relief, but lately it was difficult for her to fall asleep when a migraine began.

In November, she had a bad cold and she was constantly blowing her nose; then she couldn't hear out of her left ear. She contacted Melinda Harley, her physician and friend from high school, who prescribed a medication. A week later, Dana was still constantly blowing her nose and she still couldn't hear in her left ear. Melinda promptly referred her to an Ear, Nose and Throat (ENT) specialist and had her nurse make an appointment for that afternoon.

It was a rare sunny day, though cold, when she headed to the ENT's office. She really didn't have any thoughts about the visit other than wanting to regain her hearing. It was difficult interacting with people when she couldn't hear. Often she didn't even realize that people were standing directly next to her.

The ENT's name was Dr. Sullivan. After the initial interview, he had his technician run a battery of hearing tests. He asked her to join him in his office as he was reviewing the test results. He told her that it appeared that the loss of hearing in her left ear might be permanent. Based on her tests, he wasn't able to determine what was causing the hearing loss. He referred her to Dr. Miller, an Otolaryngologist who specialized in the diagnosis and treatment of ear, nose and throat disorders. He asked his nurse to contact Dr. Miller's office and schedule an appointment. She was able to get an appointment right away so she left and headed to Dr. Miller's office, which was close by.

Dana immediately liked Dr. Miller. He was portly and if he had had a beard, he would have been a shoo-in for Santa Claus. He had great patient rapport. He reviewed the tests results that she brought from Dr. Sullivan's and compared them with the tests she had taken in his office. "Both of these tests show a lower level of hearing than normal. I want you to return to my office next week and I'll retest you then."

His warm demeanor calmed her down. On the way home, she was able to deal with the fact that she might lose the ability to hear in her left ear. It had been weeks since she last heard in her left ear and things could have been worse. She didn't want to scare her parents, so she didn't tell them anything when she arrived home, but she did tell Bob later that evening.

She spoke with Jackie over the weekend and told her what was happening. Jackie was concerned, "This is weird; you've never had any problems with your hearing. Now they are saying that you might lose your hearing permanently. That seems like an awfully quick diagnosis."

"I don't like it either, but in the short time that I met with Dr. Miller, I feel that he'll do everything he can to save my hearing."

She returned to see Dr. Miller exactly a week later, and he immediately retested her hearing. When he came in the examining room to meet with her, he had a grave look on his face. He showed her a chart, pointed to the level that her hearing was the previous week, and then showed her where it was today. Even she could see that it had decreased substantially.

He said, "I've asked my nurse to contact the hospital and have you admitted immediately."

Before she could respond, he said, "You have some type of infection in your inner ear and I need to perform surgery as soon as possible to see if there's any way to save your hearing."

Dana was speechless, *Hospital? Operation?*

"I'll have my nurse make the arrangements, but in the meantime, who do you want my staff to contact?"

Dana immediately thought about Bob. She hadn't told her parents about the doctor's appointment since she thought it was something that would clear up quickly. It was early in the afternoon so she caught Bob at home. She quickly filled him in on what was happening.

"What's the address? I'll be there right away."

By the time Bob arrived, the nurse had arranged her admission at Good Samaritan Hospital.

"Thanks. I'll take her." By the time they reached his car, Dana was in tears.

He reached over, held her, and said, "Everything's going to be okay."

The admission process went relatively smooth. As soon as she was settled in her room, Bob left to go to her parent's home and tell them what was happening.

From then on, things moved quickly. A technician delivered an oxygen tank to her room right after Bob left. He explained how the oxygen tank worked, placed a mask over her face and she began receiving straight oxygen. The oxygen was an attempt to dry up her ear infection, but it immediately caused her to have an excruciating headache.

Dr. Miller stopped by shortly after Bob and her parents arrived. "You'll have a CAT Scan tomorrow morning and surgery later in the day as soon as an operating room opens up. Since it's a Friday it will be busy, but something will open up."

Dana wondered, *how could she be okay less than a day ago and now be preparing for surgery?*

Her parents had arranged for Ashlee to stay overnight at a friend's home telling Dana, "We didn't tell her that you're in the hospital."

Her parents left early and told her they would be back first thing the following morning. Bob assured them that he would arrange to get Dana's car home later. "In the meantime, I'll stay with her until she falls asleep." They talked and watched TV until she finally drifted off to sleep.

The next morning, Bob was the first face she saw. He had gone home, taken a brief nap, showered, changed and returned before she awoke.

Shortly after he arrived, the nurse notified her that they would be taking her down to the radiology department for a CAT Scan within the hour. When the aide arrived, Bob accompanied her down for the test, holding her hand. When she entered radiology, she looked around the room, at the large circular CAT Scan machine as they moved her from the hospital bed onto the exam table. A technician explained the procedure while making sure that she was in the proper position.

As he exited the room, he told her, "Stay absolutely still. I'll be in another room, but if you feel any discomfort, let me know. I'll be able to hear you."

The test went amazingly fast and soon she was back in her room, waiting for the nurses to let them know what time surgery would be performed.

Her parents arrived shortly after that and she could see they were concerned. Then a nurse came in, removed the oxygen tank, and started to take it out of the room. Dana asked if it was time for the surgery, and the nurse responded, "I don't think so. Dr. Miller will be in to talk to you shortly."

They were puzzled, but sat and waited. Later her mom told her that when Dr. Miller entered the room; she could tell by his face that something was wrong. He sat on the bed next to Dana with her parents and Bob close by.

"Dana, I won't be performing surgery on you today. The results of the CAT Scan revealed that you have a massive brain tumor on the left side of your brain pressing on the left ear nerve. It is causing you not to hear in your left ear. I reviewed the medical papers you completed at my office, and I saw that you've been experiencing migraines for about five years. Based on that information and the location of the tumor in your brain it's probable that the tumor is the cause of the migraines. I've already contacted Dr. Thomas, a noted neurosurgeon, who I work closely with in cases like this and his staff is arranging an appointment for you. Right now, I'm going to sign your release papers and you can go home. My office will be following up with you and Dr. Thomas."

Before he left, he asked if they had any questions. They were shocked and didn't really know what to ask.

He stopped at the door before he left and said, "You will be in good hands." They sat there in silence.

As Dana got into the car with Bob, he kept assuring her that everything was going to be okay, but she didn't believe him. Her intuition told her that this would get much worse. She closed her eyes, feigning sleep, but she was actually having a conversation with God, *Why me?*

On Monday afternoon, Dana, Bob and her parents met with Dr. Thomas, who had a matter-of-fact demeanor as he explained her situation. She had a Cholesteatoma a rare brain tumor; a benign growth of skin in an abnormal location such as the middle ear. Based on what he saw on the CAT Scan, she was probably born with it. The good news was that it was not cancerous; the bad news was it was located around vital nerves. He wanted to perform surgery as soon as possible, but first he needed her to have an Angiogram to determine if there was an aneurysm. Since the procedure required going into an artery she would need to stay overnight in the hospital. In the meantime, he would have his staff assemble the surgical team and schedule the procedure.

He told her that she would probably lose her hearing permanently. Finally, he said, "I advise you to have a will drawn up since I'm not sure if you will survive the surgery."

Dana felt like she was having a nightmare that kept getting worse and worse. In less than three weeks, she was ready for surgery, and she was at peace. It was amazing how much she learned about being sick in that short period. She had gone through the excruciating pain of the Angiogram, with dye injected in her artery, which traveled to her brain to determine if there was an aneurysm. It felt like someone poured acid in her brain, but fortunately there was no aneurysm.

Soon she felt like she had gone back to school to get a degree in the medical field. She even knew the terminology, all the required pre-tests, that the surgical team would only perform the surgery if they had all the best conditions. They wanted a particular anesthesiologist and a particular surgical room. She knew that they were doing everything possible to make her surgery a success. More importantly, she had prayer teams in her community and across the country praying for her, people that she had never met, but who had heard about her through friends and associates.

Dana swiftly went through an accelerated version of the five step grief process, common for people encountering major medical problems. First, she was in denial, and then she was angry. She was so angry at God that she actually walked out of church the first Sunday she attended after her diagnosis. After all, she thought, *if there is a God, where is He now? I'm only thirty years old, how can He do this to me?*

Then she asked for forgiveness and tried bargaining; she'd do anything if she could live to see Ashlee complete high school. She went through depression, even shutting Ashlee out for a while because it was too painful not knowing if she would see her daughter grow up. Finally, she reached acceptance. She had done everything that she could do. Jackie prepared her will and established a trust for Ashlee. Her parents would have guardianship of Ashlee, with assistance from Jackie and Dana's brothers, if she didn't survive.

Dr. Thomas stopped by her room to check on her the night before the surgery and he looked worn.

"This is much higher than us," Dana told him. "Do your best, but if there's a problem, don't let me live if I'm going to be a vegetable. Please take that extra step that will take me out of here. Now, go get some sleep, I'm okay."

As she lay in the hospital bed that night, she had a remarkable sense of inner peace, knowing and accepting that what would be would be.

# Chapter 30

When Dana came to, she was lying in a hospital room with a tube down her throat. She tried to remove the tube from her throat. Her mom was sitting close by and she reached over, and gently moved her hands away. She drifted off to sleep. When she awoke again, the tube was no longer in her throat, but she had a severe sore throat. She could see Bob sitting in the chair next to the bed and he smiled.

"Are you back with us?"

She smiled groggily and said, "I made it." As the realization hit her that she was alive, tears welled in her eyes.

"Yeah, you made it. You are in the Intensive Care Unit (ICU) now, you've been out for two days, but you definitely made it. You even astounded the doctors."

"Where's Ashlee?"

"She's at your mom's with Jackie. It's late and your parents went home to get some rest. Oh, and by the way, I'm your brother since only relatives are admitted in ICU." She smiled and drifted back to sleep.

The next day she awoke again and this time she was able to stay awake long enough to talk to her parents. There was an IV in her right arm and when she moved her head, the gauzy material from the surgical cap scratched her pillow. She asked her mom for a mirror and removed the surgical cap. She was surprised; it wasn't nearly as bad as she expected. They had shaved the left side of her head, and she could see the sutures, but they weren't as scary as she would have imagined. In all honesty, she didn't care; she was glad to be alive; to know that God had answered her prayers to stay alive to raise her daughter.

Dr. Thomas came by and told her that they would be moving her from the ICU and putting her on a neurological ward for a few more days.

"The surgery went extremely well and I was able to save your hearing. I have you on Dilantin, an anti-seizure medication, as a precautionary measure. But we'll discuss all this when you're a little stronger and before you're released."

"I have this really bad headache; an eleven on a scale of one to ten."

"It's the sutures. They'll come out in two days."

All she could do was say, "Thank you so much."

After she was moved from ICU and into her room, she began to feel better and was able to bathe with the assistance of a nurse. Her parents planned to bring Ashlee to see her as soon as she was better. She called one of her cousins who was a barber and asked him to come to the hospital and shave off her remaining hair. Her head was already hurting; there was no way she wanted to deal with touching her head, much less combing her hair anytime in the near future. She would wear a scarf until her hair grew back.

Jackie was the first person to visit her when she moved to the neurological ward. She was crying when she walked into the room.

"I'm alive, Jackie, not dead…yet. Why are you crying?"

"I'm sorry," Jackie said, trying to form a smile. "You have no idea what it's been like for all of us. None of us had any experience with being in a waiting room for a surgery like this. It was so long, although the doctor kept sending a nurse out to give us periodic updates. Then they put you in ICU, which sounded scary and dangerous. Everyone has been a nervous wreck. We've been best friends, no, sisters, for so long, I'm crying because I still have my best friend."

"Calm down, I'm okay. I'm happy that you've been here with my family, especially for Ashlee. My parents told me you have been a godsend to them."

She was released later that week and Dr. Thomas said he'd need to do at least one more surgery since he wasn't able to remove the entire tumor. He wanted to wait at least six months to allow her time to heal and to get her strength back. At the hospital, she had already begun to walk with assistance, and she felt good.

At home, it was an entirely different situation she was exhausted. Her parents gave her their downstairs bedroom, because of the heavy medications she was taking, and all she did was sleep. When Melinda, her primary physician, stopped by to see her, she told her about the fatigue. Melinda explained that it was to be expected. She told her that with the type of surgery she had it would take months before the anesthesia was completely out of her system and she started to feel like her old self again.

Jackie stayed two weeks after the surgery, helping with Ashlee and assisting her parents. She left in time to go to

Virginia to be with Gran for the Christmas holidays. By the time she left, Dana was starting to get back on her feet. Bob was visiting every day and doing everything he could to help. Since they were approaching the holidays, he and Jackie had done all the Christmas shopping for Ashlee.

Dana no longer practiced Catholicism, but on Christmas Eve, she told her parents she wanted to attend midnight Mass with them. It was a tradition that they had done most of her life; one she still enjoyed. Bob accompanied them, and as usual, it was a beautiful ceremony. A number of people she grew up with attended the service, so it was like a homecoming.

When they got home, her parents immediately went to bed saying they needed to get a few hours of sleep before Ashlee woke up. Dana and Bob sat talking in the living room looking at the Christmas tree, which she admitted her family had gone overboard with this year, when Bob said, "I have something for you."

"I thought we agreed not to exchange Christmas gifts since I wasn't able to go shopping."

"It's not a Christmas gift."

He got off the couch and walked over to the hall closet where he had hung his winter coat and removed a small jewelry box from his pocket.

"I'm not sure what order to do this in, but will you marry me?"

"Bob! What a surprise! We haven't been dating that long."

"We haven't been dating officially, but think of all the time we've spent together. Dana, I'm absolutely certain that you are the person I want to marry."

Dana knew that Bob was the perfect choice for her and that she loved him, but not in the heart throbbing way that she had with Michael or Cameron. He had been with her throughout the entire surgery, and he had seen her at her worst; yet he still wanted to marry her. He was a kind, thoughtful, caring person and he was great with Ashlee. She knew even then that he loved her unconditionally. This time she wanted a relationship that was solid, and she knew that she would have that with Bob.

"I want to say yes, but do you realize what you're getting yourself into? The doctors have already told me I have to have at least one more surgery, if not more. Based on the type of tumor I have, even after another surgery, it will probably grow back again. Are you sure you want to become part of this world?"

"I know exactly what I'm getting into. I'm getting into marrying the woman I love and forming a family with her and her daughter. If this is a yes from you, I think it's time for you to open the box."

She smiled at him as she quickly opened the jewelry box. Inside was a beautiful diamond engagement ring that fit perfectly.

"How did you know my size?"

"I asked Jackie to get me one of your rings so I'd get the size right."

"Does Jackie know about this?"

"No. I told her I was buying you a birthstone ring for Christmas."

They decided to wait until Christmas dinner before they made the announcement. Bob wanted Ashlee to enjoy her Christmas morning, and he wanted Dana to discuss their pending marriage with her before they announced their engagement.

"Ashlee's had a lot thrust on her the last few months, I want her to be comfortable with us marrying and more importantly, want me to become her stepfather."

They stayed up talking and planning for their wedding. Dana drifted off to sleep, lying in his arms, thinking, *this is one of my best Christmases, not only did I survive the surgery, but I'm engaged to a wonderful man!*

Bob didn't get a chance to make the announcement at dinner. As soon as Dana spoke to Ashlee, she went running down the stairs excitedly telling her grandparents, "My mommy's going to marry Mr. Bob, and he's going to be my dad."

Bob wasn't there because he had left after Ashlee opened her gifts to visit relatives. Dana wasn't able to contact him to let him know that Ashlee had already made the announcement.

Ashlee answered the door when Bob arrived for dinner and told him, in a matter of fact way, "Mr. Bob, you can marry my mom," which left everyone smiling.

Bob responded, "Ashlee, thank you so much because I can't do it without your approval."

1984

# Chapter 31

The following months went smoothly and Dana returned to work. Dr. Thomas scheduled her next surgery for early April and gave her the same warning, "Remember, you're still not out of danger, you need to make sure your will is up to date."

Dana was anxious, but nothing like the first time. She made all the necessary arrangements and continued with her prayer, *Please allow me to stay alive for Ashlee.*

The surgery was relatively short in comparison to the first one and when the surgery was over, Dr. Thomas immediately came out to meet with her family and Bob. He explained that he had been able to remove more of the tumor, but because of the location, decided not to go any further.

"Unfortunately, I touched the seventh nerve, the facial nerve which is very unpredictable. Sometimes you can literally hit it, and nothing will happen, other times you can barely touch the nerve, and it will result in facial palsy. Sometimes the damage is temporary, other times permanent, which cannot be determined immediately. Right now, Dana has facial palsy on the left side, whether it's temporary or permanent will not be known for a while."

Her mom asked how the palsy could be alleviated. Dr. Thomas explained that there are exercises and massages that have been successful in some cases, which he would recommend, but each case is different.

"Right now," he said, "we need to get her through recovery and address the facial palsy when she's better. I wanted to forewarn you so you won't be too shocked when you first see her."

Dana awoke and all she could see were white sheets around her. She thought she was in the morgue, until she began to see movement around her and heard talking. She realized that she was actually in the recovery room. She drifted off to sleep again. When she came to she was in a hospital room and she immediately knew it wasn't ICU. Her mom was sleeping in a chair close to her bed, but she awoke as soon as she felt Dana stir.

"Baby, how are you feeling?"

Dana said, "I'm okay, but what day is it?"

"It's Tuesday."

"I've been out a week?"

"No, you had surgery earlier today. It's 10:30 p.m. now." Her mother asked if she needed anything and then a nurse walked into the room. Dana told her she was thirsty.

"It's too soon for you to have fluids, but I will get you some ice chips. Try a few at a time; you don't want to get sick."

She was groggy, but accepted the ice chips when the nurse returned. Unfortunately, she was immediately sick to her stomach and threw up. Her mother helped her clean up and she fell asleep again.

The next morning, when she awoke, she was alone. When the nurse came in, she told Dana that her family had called and they would be there shortly. Right after the nurse left, Dr. Thomas entered the room and explained what had happened during the surgery. He reminded her that they had discussed the possibility of touching the facial nerve. Dana asked how bad it was and he reached for a mirror near her nightstand and handed it to her.

She was shocked; her face looked like she had had a stroke. All of the facial muscles on the left side of her face seemed to sag; moving down towards the ground: her eyelids, the skin on her cheekbone, her nose and even her chin.

"Is this permanent?"

"I don't know yet, I'll try everything possible to regenerate the nerve."

"I prayed for you to save my life and you did, but I never expected this."

"I know. I am very sorry."

"I'll be okay; but right now I need a little time to myself."

"Sure, I will check back on you later this evening."

She reached for the mirror, but decided she wasn't ready to look at her face again, not right now. As she lay in bed, she thought if someone had asked her what she liked about her body the most, it would have been her smile. Now she wasn't sure if she'd have it anymore. Bob and her parents arrived soon after Dr. Thomas left, and they could tell she had been crying.

Her mother tried to comfort her, "It's not that bad, honey. You still look beautiful to us."

After her parents left, Bob asked her to look directly at him. "You've avoided looking at me all day, Dana. I know this is a blow for you. I'm not going to tell you that the facial palsy doesn't exist, but I will tell you it doesn't matter. I love you for who you are. If the facial palsy is corrected, fine, but if it isn't, nothing will change as far as I'm concerned. I still love you and want to marry you as soon as possible. Now, if you will scoot over a little in that bed, maybe I can do what I really want to do right now, which is to hold you."

She had a much shorter recuperation period this time. She was released from the hospital five days after the surgery. She worked diligently massaging her face daily, but nothing stimulated the nerve. Finally, Dr. Thomas told her, "The probability is slim, based on the time that has passed, that the nerve will regenerate."

She finally accepted what happened when she realized that her prayers, to be alive to raise Ashlee, had been answered. If the facial palsy was the price she had to pay, then so be it. As the months went by, she became more comfortable with it, but she could see the initial shock when she encountered people she hadn't been in contact with recently.

She and Bob were married in September in a small ceremony with only close friends and relatives in attendance. Ashlee loved it because she was the flower girl.

Dana was perplexed at the end of the ceremony when the minister asked Ashlee to join them at the altar. Ashlee walked to the altar, stood between them and Bob lifted her up. He asked the minister to hand him some papers and said, "These are Ashlee's final adoption papers and I feel that as her father, it is proper that I make my vows to her. I vow to always be your dad, to be there for you in sickness and in health, to support you and help you in any way I can to further your development until death do we part."

Ashlee hugged him and gave him a kiss on the cheek before she said, "Okay."

There was not one dry eye in the church at the end of the ceremony.

Dana was self-conscious about taking the wedding photos. Bob hired an experienced photographer who was sensitive to her facial palsy and did an excellent job, taking most shots from her right side.

They enjoyed a honeymoon in Niagara Falls, Canada, and when they returned, they moved into Bob's home, where Jackie had already decorated Ashlee's bedroom.

*1985*

# *Chapter 32*

Jackie remained living in the Bay Area much longer than she originally planned. During that time, she honed her skills in the Estate and Gift field. As part of her strategic plan to become as marketable as possible, she decided to pursue her Master's in Business Administration (MBA) in Taxation. She was accepted at Golden Gate University, which had an excellent night program. She was extremely busy, but she genuinely enjoyed her chosen field and she could honestly say, without boasting, that she was exceptionally good at what she did.

Nearly four years ago she developed a strategic career plan, and thanks to her hard work, and Matt, who turned out to be a great mentor, she had reached a critical milestone. Earlier in the month, she interviewed with the key partners at Stevens, Laramie, Zuckerman and Wilson, Attorneys at Law. She spent two days at their office. During that time, she took a tour of the firm, met with various managers, all of whom were evaluating her to see if she would be a good fit for the firm. Today she was extremely happy; she had received a call from Franklin offering her a mid level position with the firm, at a salary much higher than she anticipated.

As soon as she ended her conversation with Franklin, she picked up the phone to contact the leasing company and let them know she would no longer be renting the townhouse. It was perfect timing since the current tenant's lease would expire in 60 days. She had negotiated a 30-day reporting date with a 90-day housing allowance with the firm. She would stay in a hotel until the unit was vacated and refurbished.

When she finished the call, the next person she contacted was Matt, then Dana, and finally, Aunt Mildred. She waited until she got home to call Gran because she knew they would be talking for a long time.

Two weeks later Jackie left Baldwin & Baldwin after they held a lavish going away luncheon in her honor and she flew directly to Cincinnati. Dana was planning a big birthday party for Ashlee's seventh birthday, which she was looking forward to attending. Dana originally planned to have the party at her home, but changed her plans since it was so hot. She decided to hold a swimming and slumber party instead at a local hotel for Ashlee and some of her closest friends.

Some of the girls' parents stayed for a while, so for the adults it was a relaxing afternoon spent sitting around the pool and talking. Dana had reserved two adjoining suites at the hotel, one for the girls and one for them. The girls had a blast; swimming all day, enjoying pizza, taking a rest and returning to the pool to swim until it closed. After the girls swam, Jackie and Dana helped them with their showers and got them settled down in their room with popcorn and a movie. Jackie was amazed at the amount of energy the kids had and finally asked Dana if they ever got tired.

"Eventually, but that's a win-lose situation because they'll rest and then it starts all over again."

While the girls were engrossed in the movie, Jackie and Dana had time to talk. Jackie filled her in on everything about her new job, including the fact that the firm had mailed her numerous packages to familiarize herself with before she started.

"Sounds like it will be a lot of work."

"It will be, but I did my Master's program while I was establishing Baldwin & Baldwin's Trust Department and that was a lot of pressure with school and work deadlines. I think I'm up for it. I have to keep my eye on the prize - making partner by the time I reach 45."

Dana laughed and said, "Somehow I think that's a given."

Dana continued, "I've been meaning to tell you, I'm looking for a new job."

"Why? I thought you enjoyed your job at the nursing home."

"I do," said Dana. "But I need to be realistic. Dr. Thomas has already told me that he'll probably have to do another surgery next year. The nursing home is too small to handle an employee who is away from work as often as I am, even if it is due to illness."

"So have you considered what you want to do?

"I'd like to try social work, so I applied to Hamilton County Social Services and I have an interview next week."

"That sounds like a good idea. They'll be lucky to have you."

"I don't have the job yet."

"But you will," said Jackie.

As they continued talking, they discussed the fact that Bob and Dana would be celebrating their first wedding anniversary in two months.

Dana said, "I can't believe it's been almost a year."

"Bob's a good man."

"He is and I almost blew it."

"Really, how?"

"Well, initially I thought that since I wasn't having the bells and whistles, and my heart wasn't beating like it had with Michael and Cameron, maybe Bob wasn't the one. Then I had a reality check. That's all I had with Michael was bells and whistles, except for Ashlee. Dana paused, "Cameron...well... that wasn't to be. Bob has been the best person I could have ever married. He's a caring, supportive husband. I know he'll always be there for me and he's been such a great dad for Ashlee. I've been very fortunate."

Jackie said, "Today when I watched Ashlee in the pool, it was like I was looking at Michael. Does she ever ask about him?"

"You're right she does look like her dad. To answer your question, she doesn't ask about Michael. I've told her about him and she even has a few pictures of him. She was so young when we left Oakland and she never knew her dad so to her, Bob is her father."

"You ever hear anything about Michael?"

"Not recently. His brother, Aaron, went to California and located him right after we left the Bay Area, but he was still an addict living on the streets. There was nothing he could do to persuade Michael to get help. Aaron said he looked horrible and it was terrible to see him like that. He gave him his phone number and told him if he ever wanted to get clean to give him a call, but he hasn't heard anything from him. Aaron and his wife, Sarah, have been great about staying in contact with Ashlee. They live in Dallas now and are expecting their second child soon. They met Bob when they were here last year for

Michael's dad's funeral. They really hit it off and they invited us out to visit them. We all want the kids to know each other, so we're thinking about a trip next year."

"What about Cameron?"

"Not a word. It's painful for me to even think about him, Jackie. Can you believe it? After all that's happened. But... what about you? Do you ever hear anything about Gary?"

"Not really. Last year I was at a fundraiser in San Francisco, and I ran into Lisa, the wife of one of the players. I was friendly with her when I was married. She tried to find out why I left Gary, but I told her things were not working out. Then she told me how Gary was now a big star on the team. She went on and on about how I devastated him and that he hadn't dated much since I left. She said he now spends most of his time with this best friend, Jarvis, who is a well known New York disc jockey."

"How did you react to that?"

"I kept a solemn face and said, 'well, I hope that everything will work out for him.' Then I said, 'Excuse me, I see my friend, who I'm supposed to meet, just arrived.' All the time, I was thinking, *if you only knew*, but there was no way I was going to do or say anything for her to repeat."

"You've talked about how your career is going and how you're on track with your plan, but how is your personal life?"

Jackie took a moment before she replied. "You know, it's funny. I am right on track to meet my goal, but sometimes there is a little sadness. I'm happy, but there seems to be something missing. When I get home after a major accomplishment, I usually end up feeling melancholy. You and my family are supportive, but there are times when I wish I were in a committed relationship. I wish there was someone at home to celebrate my successes with, but that's not in the cards for me now. Thank goodness, the sadness doesn't last long. Just like it starts, it's over, and I'm okay again. I'm not sure what that's about, but right now, I'm not going to focus on it. I'm staying on track to make partner."

The movie ended and the girls came in to see if they could play a game.

Dana said, "Hold on, I'll be in there shortly."

She told Jackie, "I'll shut the door so you can get some sleep, looks like they'll be up quite a while." She left the room, and Jackie prepared for bed, thinking, *I don't know how she does it.*

The following day, Jackie left to visit Gran. She was always surprised when she saw Gran who had shrunk over the years. She was in good health and walked thirty minutes every day when the weather was good. During their time together, Jackie slept in late and awoke to Gran in the kitchen cooking breakfast.

One day, Gran made a comment, "It looks to me like you haven't been getting enough rest by the way you're sleeping late every day. I'm so proud of you; you've done so well, but be careful not to make work your whole life."

"Well, the last few years have been rough, and I haven't always gotten enough rest, but I was working on my MBA and starting a new department at the firm. Now that I have my Master's, I should be able to get a little more rest."

Over the years, Jackie and Aunt Mildred made minor changes to Gran's house. Now, as she looked around, she realized that the house needed some renovations. She contacted Charles Adkins, an old high school classmate of hers who was a contractor, to come out and look at the house. Charles told her that the house, although old, was in solid shape. He recommended that she purchase safety items for the house designed to assist the elderly, like a grab bar in the bathtub, stair railings for the porch, and outside security lights.

She asked him to purchase all the items he recommended and any others he thought would be useful at the house. Then she took Gran shopping to purchase paint, carpet and new furniture. Gran kept protesting that she was doing too much. Finally, Jackie told her she had received two substantial bonuses. One was a sign-on bonus from Stevens, Laramie, Zuckerman, and Wilson. The other from Baldwin & Baldwin for the outstanding job she had done in establishing their Trust Department.

Before she left, she hired Charles to oversee the work; ensuring it would be completed correctly and timely.

Gran was so happy, she said, "I feel like I'm moving into a new house."

The following Sunday, Jackie prepared to start her new position. She made sure that she went to bed early, and had all her clothes ready for the next day. On Monday morning at exactly 7:50 a.m., she arrived at Stevens, Laramie, Zuckerman, and Wilson, Attorneys at Law, and took the elevator to the fourth floor.

*1996*

# Chapter 33

Dana often found herself thinking; *it's amazing how quickly time passes as we get older*. Following their marriage, she and Bob soon fell into an easy routine. Bob completed his Master's program the following year and accepted a position as Chief Financial Officer of their suburban Cincinnati community. Based on his military experience and his involvement in the community, he was an excellent choice for the position and he definitely enjoyed his work.

Initially, they lived in the small ranch style house where Bob was raised. Shortly after moving in, they realized that it was too small for them and decided to rent it out. They had a four-bedroom house custom built in the community that they grew up in and they loved their home. A friend was an interior decorator, so she helped them decorate the interior and it was exactly what they wanted. They discovered that they both had a knack for gardening, and as a result, they spent a great deal of time doing yard work, often competing with neighbors to see who had the most original landscape. They planned to take Master Gardener classes when Ashlee was in college.

Financially they were in a good position, and with the exception of her surgeries, they were doing great. Two years ago, Dr. Thomas had to sever her hearing in her left ear in order to remove the remaining tumor. She accepted the loss knowing that there were no other options.

Dana currently worked as a social worker for Hamilton County Social Services, and she enjoyed her work, although it was trying sometimes. She assisted applicants in the intake area with completing the required paperwork. Primarily the clients were young single mothers with a child, or a child on the way, and they were overwhelmed with the paperwork. Many of them didn't have a clue to what needed to be done nor a plan for their future or that of a child.

Today, she and Bob had met with Dr. Thomas to discuss her most recent Magnetic Resonance Imaging (MRI) results. He informed her that there was no sign of the tumor and she would not need to have another MRI, or meet with him for three years. They were ecstatic. Ten plus years and five surgeries, which had left her mentally and physically drained each time, but her constant prayer to be alive and to raise Ashlee, had been answered.

They went to dinner that evening to celebrate the good news and neither of them was sleepy when they returned home. They were lying in bed talking and waiting as they usually did to hear the garage door open, signaling that Ashlee was home.

"You know, Ashlee could actually open the garage door and not enter the house, and we'd never know since we usually fall asleep as soon as we hear it open."

Bob shook his head and smiled, "You're right."

Dana asked, "Do you ever think we made the wrong decision?"

"About what?"

"Well, not to have children."

"Dana, you know I don't go back and relive the past and try to make it different than what it was. We made the best decision for us at the time. I'm not going to tell you that I wouldn't have wanted to have a child with you, but Dr. Thomas explained that the nature of the tumor was that it was similar to a weed. It would continue to grow unless they removed every shred. He told us to be prepared for you to have additional surgeries since he wanted to be cautious and tread lightly, as not to damage other vital organs. With the thought of you having additional surgeries, and the risks associated with each surgery, we decided that I'd have a vasectomy before we got married. I know it was the best decision for us. I'm okay with our decision, but it sounds like you're having some regrets about it."

"No, not really, it's probably more about Ashlee graduating this year and thinking how it's going to be so quiet around here. Maybe it's premature empty nesters syndrome."

"Don't worry about that, we'll be okay."

Right then, they heard the garage door open. When Ashlee came upstairs she could see the light from their bedroom and hear them talking, so she knocked on the door.

When she entered the room she asked, "What are you guys doing up so late?"

Dana said, "Talking."

"About what?"

Her mom answered, "Things in general."

"But why?" asked Ashlee.

"Oh, it's one of those things parents do sometimes while waiting for their daughter to get home," Bob said.

"Okay, Dad, I wasn't late. I learned the hard way that you don't play about curfews. The time I blew it, I didn't think I'd ever get off punishment."

"It was only a month."

"Well, since you're up, how about this? I talked to Aunt Jackie while you were at dinner tonight and asked her if she would help me get a job this summer in DC, maybe as a junior Congressional aide. I could stay with her, if that's okay with you."

Bob said, "Jackie works long hours, I'm not sure if that would work, but we can discuss it later."

"Really?" Dana asked. "That sounds interesting, but what did Jackie say?"

"She said it's okay with her, but she needed to discuss it with both of you."

"Okay." After Ashlee left their room, Dana asked Bob, "How do you feel about Ashlee staying with Jackie this summer?"

"I don't have any problem with it, but I'm not sure how it will be for Jackie the way she works."

"I don't know how she's kept her pace for this long, but you know it's her goal to make partner by the time she's 45, and she's on track to make it. She's going to continue working long hours until she makes partner."

"I know Jackie wants to spend some one-on-one time with Ashlee," Dana continued. "You have to give it to her; she's been an exceptional godmother. Think about how she never missed a recital, or major swimming competition, or any of the other activities that suited Ashlee's fancy."

Bob laughed and said, "You're right, and she enjoyed every one of them."

"One time she told me that she made a conscious decision to make her career her life. She said she was okay with her decision because I allowed her to share, in part, in raising Ashlee. She could honestly say she didn't have any regrets. She felt like she had part of both worlds."

Dana began yawning, "I'm going to sleep. I'll talk to Jackie about this later this week. We've still got a few months before Ashlee graduates."

The day of Ashlee's graduation, Dana got to the airport earlier than planned so she decided to walk down to the gate to meet Jackie's flight. When she reached the gate, Jackie was the first passenger off the plane.

They hugged, and Jackie's first question was, "Where's my girl?"

"She had left to go to the hairdresser when I got up, but I'm sure that she'll be home when we arrive."

On the way home, they talked about the weekend plans, including the graduation that evening and the party at their home the next day.

Jackie asked, "Is she excited?"

Dana glanced at her briefly and said, "You tell me."

"Bouncing off the walls," said Jackie.

"Exactly," said Dana, and they both laughed.

"You have another celebration coming up soon, don't you?"

Dana said, "Actually two celebrations, my 43rd birthday and our 12th wedding anniversary."

Jackie jokingly said, "Girl, you know you're getting old."

"You're right, but you're a few months older than me, so I think we're in the same boat."

Jackie said, "You're right."

"But back to your question, we haven't made any plans yet. We are going to wait until after the graduation and then do all the things for Ashlee that we need to finish before she leaves for college. We will probably do something in the fall when she's away at college."

"Are you guys okay with becoming empty nesters?"

"We've talked about it and know it will definitely be quieter, some days that sounds like a plus."

"How are you doing, still on track to make partner by 45?"

Jackie hesitated before she said, "No, not really."

Dana glanced at her and asked, "Did I hear you right?"

"Yeah, you heard me right. I'm no longer on track to make partner by 45. I officially became a partner at Stevens, Laramie, Zuckerman and Wilson, Attorneys at Law, yesterday."

"What? Oh, my God, that's wonderful! When were you were going to tell me?"

"I wanted to wait until after Ashlee's graduation. This is her special weekend and I don't want to intrude on her big event."

"Oh, no, we will be celebrating your partnership this weekend too."

At the graduation later that evening, Dana cried throughout the ceremony.

She and Jackie had driven together while Bob dropped her parent's at home. Jackie asked her, "Are you okay?"

Dana told her, "Yes. I've never told you, or anyone else, but for the last twelve years, I have prayed every day that I'd be here to see Ashlee graduate. Tonight I am definitely more than okay."

The graduation party went great the next day. It was an all day event with a catered barbeque. There was a continuous flow of guests throughout the day and early evening. Later, Ashlee and her friends went to another party. Dana, Bob and Jackie sat in the family room catching up, but first they did a toast to Jackie making partner.

"I'm really sorry that Gran couldn't be here this weekend," Bob said.

"Yes, I know," Jackie said. "But she hasn't been feeling well. Aunt Mildred's in Virginia with her now and I'm going there for a few days when I leave here. We're going to try to convince her to move with us."

Dana said, "Good luck."

"I know what you mean; we probably have a better chance of moving Grand Canyon than we do of moving Gran."

# Chapter 34

Jackie was sitting in the first class cabin and sipping a glass of champagne on her flight to Virginia. She closed her eyes, and smiled for a moment, recalling Franklin's announcement during the staff meeting. "Stevens, Laramie, Zuckerman, and Wilson, Attorneys at Law, consider many qualities in selecting potential partners. We look for intelligence, thorough knowledge of the law, quickness, and common sense. We expect integrity, solid client relationships, and a good business sense, stability in both personal and professional life. In the case of our firm, we also want absolute dedication to the firm and our work. I can happily say that we have all of that, and much more, in Jackie Colson. Without further ado, I'd like to welcome her as our newest senior partner."

There was a round of applause and then each partner came over to shake her hand and congratulate her. She was on top of the world. She kept thinking, *I made it,* as she accepted congratulations.

When she returned to her office, the staff had heard about her selection as senior partner and many stopped by to say congratulations. Finally, she was able to get up from her desk and close the door so she could call Gran. Aunt Mildred answered the phone and she told her, "I have some news for both of you and I'd like to tell you at the same time, so do you mind getting the extension for Gran?" When they were both on the phone, she told them, "You are now talking to the newest senior partner at Stevens, Laramie, Zuckerman, and Wilson, Attorneys at Law."

They were so excited for her. Gran said, "Baby, I am so proud of you."

The firm had a tradition when they selected a new partner; they went out for dinner the night of the announcement to celebrate. In keeping with that tradition, they went out immediately following work, so it was after 9:00 p.m. when Jackie arrived at home. She was startled by the flight attendant who asked for her champagne flute, saying, "We're about to start the landing process," bringing her back to the present.

She shook her head slightly, now she had other things she needed to deal with. Gran was turning eighty-one this year and she was adamant that she didn't want to leave her home and move with them, or anywhere else. She was still spry and active, and the neighbors watched out for her, but she and Aunt Mildred worried about her living alone. Last night, Bob recommended getting her a medical alert bracelet and having someone come in to assist her with cleaning and shopping as needed.

She thought it was a good idea and planned to discuss those options with Gran and Aunt Mildred tonight, since Aunt Mildred would be leaving the following day. Her biggest problem would be convincing Gran to get someone to come in to help her.

Gran was definitely doing much better because she was in the kitchen cooking when Jackie arrived. Jackie could smell the aroma of food as soon as she entered the house and knew Gran had made all of her favorites. Gran had contacted some of her friends and they were coming by for dinner later. Before Jackie could say anything, Gran said, "You know I believe in celebrating events and this is a big one; and one you've been working on for years. We will definitely celebrate; my grandbaby is a partner in a big time law firm."

When Jackie looked over at Aunt Mildred, she shrugged her shoulders and said, "You know your grandmother."

They had a great time that evening and later when the guests left, they sat on the front porch talking. Gran surprised Jackie and Aunt Mildred when she said, "I know that both of you are concerned about me and want me to move with you, but I don't want to do that. My roots are here. I have my friends and my church here, and both of you have busy lives, so I would be by myself most of the time. My friend Emma is staying in a senior citizen's apartment now since her husband died and she's not happy there. Most of her family is gone and you know she and her husband didn't have children so we talked about her moving in here with me. She could take one of the extra bedrooms. She doesn't have much furniture so we figured we could make it work. Maybe get one of those professional organizers like I see on TV to help us."

Neither Jackie nor Aunt Mildred said a word.

"She only gets $240 a month from social security so I'm not going to charge her any rent. We figured we would split the utility bills and food since the house is paid for and both of you pay the insurance and taxes." Gran continued, "Anyway, we plan to try it for a couple of months and see how it works, and if everything is okay, she'll move in before the weather gets cold."

All they could do was say it sounded like a good idea. Jackie said, "If you decide to do it, we'll come down and help you get everything set up."

Later that evening after Gran went to bed, Jackie and Aunt Mildred talked and they both agreed that it was a good idea. Miss Emma and Gran already did a lot together, so it would probably be good for both of them.

Aunt Mildred said, "I definitely didn't see this coming."

"Neither did I, but its okay. It means that you and I will share a bedroom when we visit at the same time, but that's not an issue for me."

When Jackie returned home, she could sense the melancholy feeling coming over her as soon as she got off the plane. By the time she reached her townhouse, the sense of sadness was overwhelming. *Why am I so sad each time I attain a goal?*

She knew something was missing for her. She had continued moving up at the firm, getting one promotion after another, purchasing property, and making good financial investments. Unfortunately, each time she accomplished another feat, she was a little sad. She had friends who shared in her accomplishments, her family and Dana's family were definitely supportive of her, but sometimes she still wanted a relationship where she could share her success with a significant other.

One time, Gran told her, "I'm so proud of your success, baby, but don't let it be the only thing in your life. Life can get awfully lonely when you don't let others in."

Jackie dated a great deal over the years. Her position at the firm exposed her to men of many different ethnic backgrounds. She was accustomed to dating a diverse group of men from various social economic groups. She dated men who were politicians, doctors, even a personal trainer. Her basic requirement was that they had to be a good person. Most men quickly got tired of her canceling dates and always making work her number 1, 2, and 3 priority. One of her dates told her, "Jackie, you're a very attractive and intelligent woman, but serious relationships aren't as important to you as your career, so it's impossible for me to want to continue dating you."

She tried to explain that it was her dream, her lifelong goal to make partner, but even she had to acknowledge that she was a workaholic. She hoped that she would be able to reduce her hours now that she made partner, but she knew it wouldn't happen right away.

When she returned to her office, she had a telephone message from Nathaniel Evanston. She couldn't remember who he was at first. Then she remembered he was a young attorney she met while she was doing pro bono work at Legal Aid. She returned his call and he told her that he had heard through the legal grapevine that she had made partner and called to congratulate her.

"Thanks so much," she said, glancing at the paperwork on her desk while trying to figure out how to end the call quickly.

He asked, "If I'm not being too forward, can I take you out for a drink to celebrate?"

She agreed, but wasn't sure exactly why.

They met the next evening at Ralph's, a well-respected restaurant and bar that many attorneys frequented. She vaguely remembered him as he approached her, 6 feet tall, muscular build, almond-colored with a small splash of freckles across his nose. They had an enjoyable evening. Jackie found out that Nate was from North Carolina and attended Duke University for undergrad before enrolling in Howard University's law school. He was working at a small firm that handled a myriad of issues, and like her, he had been a volunteer when she met him at Legal Aid.

"That's how I started, with a small firm in Oakland and later I decided to specialize in trusts, with an emphasis in estate and gift."

When they finished drinks, Jackie told Nate, "Thanks so much, but I need to get home. I've got an early day tomorrow."

"Is it possible that we could go out again?"

"Unless I'm blind, I'm a bit older than you."

"That's not an issue for me."

"Exactly how old are you?"

"Thirty-three."

"Well, I'm exactly 10 years older than you, so I'll take a pass, that's a little out of my comfort zone."

She called Dana when she got home to let her know she had received a call from the Congressman's office to finalize the plans for Ashlee to work as a junior aide.

She said, "I'm so excited. I've already adjusted my schedule for the two weeks she'll be here, and Aunt Mildred will be my back up in an emergency."

Then she gave Dana an update on Gran's plans to have a roommate.

"That's a great idea. Bob hasn't told you yet, but he's changing fields and wants to start working in the geriatric area. He has a vision to build a senior citizen's complex in the community with affordable housing, activities for seniors, transportation to medical appointments, and meals, if needed. He's working with local churches to see if they will sponsor his effort."

Jackie mentioned having drinks with Nate and she was surprised when Dana asked, "Why won't you go out with him again?"

"Because, I'm ten years older than he is."

"So, is there a problem with a woman being older than a man? You don't have a problem with Bob being ten years older than me. Sounds like a double standard to me. You said you had a nice evening, and I don't remember you mentioning dating lately. It's a date, you know, not a marriage proposal."

"Well, I told him no, so it's a moot issue now."

"Humph, we'll see."

*Chapter 35*

A shlee began her internship the third week in July. Jackie realized that it was the first time she'd had any semblance of normal work hours since Ashlee was a baby and she helped Dana take care of her. She arranged with Aunt Mildred to get Ashlee to work since she had recently retired and had a flexible morning schedule. Each day, Jackie departed her office promptly at 4:30 p.m. so she could meet Ashlee at the METRO train at 5:00 p.m.

In the evenings, they returned home or went out to eat and discussed their day. Ashlee enjoyed the internship. There were students from across the United States participating in the program so she met kids from diverse backgrounds. In addition to the work the students performed, they attended various leadership classes.

Ashlee was primarily doing filing and running errands for the staff, but she said that she loved the feel of the city and working in such an interesting environment. Occasionally she would see a noted politician and later that night they would talk about it.

The second weekend they took the train to New York after work on Friday so they could go shopping and attend an August Wilson play. The time went by too fast for both of them. It seemed like Ashlee had just arrived and it was already time for her to return home and prepare for college.

Ashlee had been gone for over a month and Jackie was still missing her. Periodically she thought about the evening she had drinks with Nate and smiled. She had to acknowledge that she had enjoyed their evening together.

*I wonder what it would be like*, she thought, *to date a man ten years younger than me.* She knew she didn't look 43. She received enough compliments from people who were surprised at her age saying she looked like she was in her thirties, but the ten year age difference made her uncomfortable.

To her surprise, Nate called her exactly two months after they went out for drinks and asked her if she was free for lunch, not a date, he added. She smiled and said sure.

They met at a bistro close to her office and again she enjoyed his company. She found herself telling him about being raised in Virginia. Talking with him was like being with an old friend. At the end of lunch, he asked, "So, since you had lunch with me, is it possible that we could go out next week and this time make it a date?"

Jackie could hear Dana's voice and said sure.

They began dating. She loved living in the nation's capital, but she rarely took time to enjoy its vast history. Jackie knew that Nate didn't make the kind of money she did, so they took advantage of visiting the many free landmarks in the city, including the vast museums. With Nate, she saw a whole other perspective of the city. She had to acknowledge that she was having fun, something she rarely did, and laughing more than she had in years. When they finally slept together, she thought she would die from the sheer pleasure.

Winter was beginning to set in, so they spent a great deal of time together on weekends and after work at her townhouse, cooking together, talking and watching old movies. She only went to his apartment once because he shared an apartment with a roommate who, he said, spent a great deal of time at home. It was a nice, neat two- bedroom, one bath apartment close to Rock Creek Park. His roommate was out, but Nate said, "He's a hermit, he'll be home soon." He asked her if she wanted to stay over and she said no, thinking, *I am too old to even consider staying over, if it means sharing a bathroom."*

For the first time in a long while, she was happy. They were together so frequently that they decided it would make more sense if he moved in with her since he was rarely home. Nate even began attending office functions with her and he fit in comfortably in that environment.

Nate asked her to marry him during the spring of 1997, and she immediately accepted. She enjoyed being with him and she felt that they were definitely on the right path. It was also nice to have someone whom she could share her accomplishments with.

When she told Dana, she said, "I'm happy for you and I'm looking forward to meeting Nate." Then she asked, "Are you going to get a prenuptial agreement?"

"I hadn't thought about it."

"You're the attorney. You know what you need to do."

When she mentioned it to Nate, he said, "Sure, you can do that, but it sounds like you have some trust issues with me."

Jackie quickly assured him that she trusted him.

"You decide, but we definitely won't need a prenup for my assets."

Two months later, they got married at the Justice of the Peace. Jackie told Nate that she had already had an elaborate wedding and didn't want to do that again. Following the wedding, they went to the beach in Outer Banks, North Carolina. Although they had talked on the phone numerous times, Jackie had not met Nate's parents, so they went to their home after the honeymoon. His dad seemed okay, but Jackie immediately sensed that his mother didn't like her. She attempted to have a conversation with her, but she responded in gruff tones.

Finally, when they were in the kitchen preparing lunch, Jackie asked, "Did I do or say something to offend you?"

His mother turned from the kitchen sink and faced her before she answered, "No, you have not said anything to offend me, but I have a question for you. How old are you?"

"I'm forty-four."

"You're 10 years younger than Nate's dad and I. Aren't you robbing the cradle?"

"No, Nate and I are okay with our age difference. But is it an issue for you?"

"Yes, it's definitely an issue, we were looking forward to having grandkids and that probably won't happen now."

"Nate and I discussed that and we don't want to have children."

"Humph, that's not what he said last year."

Jackie was surprised, since that was one of the major points during their discussions before they got married. She thought, *he probably gave up the idea when he met me, so she decided not to discuss it with him.*

2003

# Chapter 36

Jackie had been married for six years and she was questioning her decision to marry Nate. She realized she had been at an emotional low when they began dating. She should have taken time to assess what was happening in her life instead of putting on blinders and making a snap decision to get married. She ignored Dana's suggestion to get a prenuptial agreement and now she sincerely regretted that decision.

The first two years of the marriage went relatively smoothly; they generally had a good time. They moved into a condominium, which was much larger than her townhouse. They used her money to make some real-estate investments, including purchasing property in Vail, Colorado. Nate was an avid skier, so they traveled to Vail and he taught her how to ski, although she preferred to stay in the cabin and relax while he hit the slopes.

In the third year of their marriage, Nate decided that he no longer wanted to work at the small firm he had been with for the last seven years, saying he felt he had an untapped entrepreneurial spirit. Nate had a charismatic personality, and Jackie believed that with a little work on his part, he could establish a successful business. She wanted to show her support of him, so she funded two projects over the last three years, a consulting firm for new business owners and a computer tech firm, resulting in her losing over $300K. Each of the projects could have been successful, but Nate insisted on putting too much money into overhead, having an impressive office, and taking potential customers to expensive dinners when he hadn't generated any income.

Now Nate was changing directions again and wanted to pursue politics. Recently, he had approached her about trying to run for an elected office.

"What do you know about the position; you currently need to have a full-time job, so how is that going to work?"

She suggested that he might want to explore volunteering in some political activities to get an idea of what it would be like. She could tell that he didn't like her response, but they decided to table the conversation until later. That night, when she lay in bed, she acknowledged that, in addition to the age difference, she and Nate were as different as night and day. Most of her life she knew what she wanted and went after it. Nate was the opposite, searching and floundering, not quite sure of what or where he wanted to be.

She had talked to him about trying to visualize what he wanted to do, but his response was, "I'm not like you; I'm still trying to find my way."

She did not respond, but she thought, *that would be great if you used your own money to find your way.*

For their 50th birthdays, Jackie and Dana went to Negril, Jamaica. They had both read an article about a small holistic spa coincidently named Jackie's on the Reef and were interested in trying it out.

They coordinated their flights so they arrived in Montego Bay within thirty minutes of each other. They zipped through Customs and Immigration and headed out of the airport, where a driver was waiting for them. The ride to Negril was peaceful, with the ocean to the right of them as they rode the ninety minutes to the spa.

The spa was exactly what they both envisioned: small, with sparse furnishings, and a large veranda with small beds and hammocks for guests to relax, and a breathtaking ocean view. As soon as they settled in their room, they received an island drink. The host informed them they were scheduled to get a massage in thirty minutes. They initially wanted to postpone their massage, but Ms. Lewis; the owner convinced them that a massage was exactly what they needed to rid themselves of some of their U.S. stress. They spent the next few days taking yoga classes in the morning and receiving spa treatments each day. They were amazed that they both were taking long naps during the day, obviously more tired than they realized. The spa's signature treatment was a body scrub given outdoors. The gentle pressure of the loofah brush and the scent of rosemary branches used during the treatment convinced them that they had died and gone straight to heaven.

They spent evenings sitting on the steps of the spa talking as they watched the incredible Negril sunset. One night, Jackie told Dana she wasn't happy in her marriage. She told her how much money she had lost on Nate's business ventures and that she had recently contracted a sexually transmitted disease (STD) from him.

"I don't think I've ever been as shocked or embarrassed as I was when I went to my gynecologist and she informed me I had a STD. When I got home and confronted Nate, he tried to lie about it until I pointed out that tests don't lie and I hadn't been involved with anyone but him. Then he confessed that he had been sleeping with someone for a while, but it was over. He wanted to tell me more, but I didn't want to hear it."

Dana listened quietly.

Jackie continued, "To be honest, I'm not entirely surprised." She shook her head, "What was I thinking when I decided to marry him? Why didn't you tell me not to get married?"

"Because you didn't ask, I only met Nate briefly when you came to Ohio for a weekend visit. I thought Nate was a nice enough person, but not necessarily the person for you to marry. The next thing I knew, you were announcing that you were getting married the following week. I didn't think it was my place to say maybe you should wait or reconsider. Anyway, what are you going to do?"

"I don't know. I'd like us to try marriage counseling. I think I still love him." Then she added, "I wish we were like you and Bob; you guys have a perfect relationship."

"No we don't. There is no such thing. We're like other couples we have issues sometimes. Lately, I've wanted to pursue my dream to see the world, to travel more. Bob is so busy with the senior citizen project that he doesn't want to leave. Even when we do go on a trip, he's in constant contact with his office. I knew he wasn't overly interested in traveling when I met him, but not to this extent, but this isn't a deal breaker. I love him and I respect what he does for the community, but sometimes I'd like us to have a romantic getaway." Then she laughed, "But on the positive side, he never questions how much I spend when I go on vacation with a friend, so I'll probably be travelling with you more often."

Dana asked, "Out of curiosity, why didn't you want to know any more about why Nate had an affair?"

"I guess I didn't want to hear the truth. I'm not sure if it's his infidelity, or the fact that I'm fifty, that's making me apprehensive. I'm going through menopause, with severe hot flashes and my interest in sex is declining. I didn't think I could handle his response if it dealt with my age."

"Aren't we all having age related issues? I don't get hot flashes yet, but I do get serious night sweats. I wake up in the middle of the night freezing because my pajama top is damp. I've started to leave an extra top on the night stand next to the bed; not such a great feeling. Did you ever envision either of us going through the change?"

They decided to put their problems aside and enjoy their getaway. Before they left, they promised to return the following year.

2005

# Chapter 37

Jackie filed for divorce two years later. She contacted Dana the day before she was scheduled to meet with her attorney and told her what she was going to do.

"But what happened, I thought you worked out your marriage issues."

"Not really, I was avoiding them. I got tired of complaining about a relationship when I wasn't doing anything but complaining, so I decided to quit talking about it. I am so tired of this marriage, tired of Nate's cheating, tired of being nowhere near where I was financially before we married, tired of wasting time and money on marriage counseling. This marriage is nothing but a farce. I should have filed for divorce years ago, but I let my ego get in the way, wondering what people might think. Now, I am through with this relationship, and I don't give a damn what people think. The final clincher is Nate has another family."

Up until this point, Dana had allowed Jackie to vent, but now she said, "Hold on, what did you say?"

"I said Nate has another family. Nate has a two year old son by a woman named Sharon Talbert and they are expecting another child. They live in North Carolina, interestingly enough, close to Nate's parents."

"Are you sure? How did you find all this out?"

"I'm definitely sure. I've been suspicious of his behavior for a while, but I thought Nate was having another one of his short term affairs. For the last two years, Nate has been traveling to North Carolina monthly, telling me he was helping his parents. Since I've always had a distant relationship with my now soon- to- be -ex in-laws, I didn't contact him when he was there."

"In November, I requested a credit report for both of us after Franklin informed me that he had been a victim of stolen identity. Someone was using his social security number and running up all types of credit card bills and he was having difficulty resolving the issue."

She hesitated before continuing, "I reviewed my report and I was pleased that everything looked good and no one was using my credit data. Since I had both reports, I decided to check Nate's report also, thinking it would mirror mine. When I checked, Nate had two credit cards listed in his name that were unfamiliar to me. We agreed to keep our credit cards to a maximum of two each, so I was upset about that, but then I saw that they both showed a North Carolina address. I thought it might be a mistake, so I used a special computer program the firm maintains to cross check the address for names and phone numbers of the residents. The address listed was in the names of Sharon and Nate Evanston.

"I wasn't sure exactly what Nate was doing, so I contacted Phil Eddington, a private investigator our firm keeps on retainer for our high profile divorce cases. I gave him all the information that I had, negotiated a fee for his service and asked him to be discreet with his inquiries.

"Yesterday I received Phil's report and it shows I have been married to a complete fraud. First, when I met Nate and he told me he had a roommate, it wasn't a man. It was his girlfriend, Sharon Talbert, who he's been dating off and on since college and all during our marriage. There's even a copy of the lease agreement they had at that time in the report.

"There are also pictures of the two of them together in North Carolina with their son, Sean, and all of them attending church services with his parents. In addition to the pictures, Phil provided me with copies of the current lease agreement, utility bills in their names, and joint savings and checking account information. He even included a signed copy of the baby's birth certificate."

Jackie had been talking extremely fast, but slowed down to say, "I still can't believe this. It feels like a nightmare; like déjà vu from my marriage with Gary."

Dana said, "Are you going to be okay?"

"Hell no," said Jackie. "I am livid! He told me so many lies; I don't know where to begin. What I told you is only part of the story. You should see the file that Phil put together; page after page of nothing but lies."

Dana asked, "Is there any way possible to save your marriage, or do you want to save it?"

"You couldn't give me ten million dollars to stay with him. I hired Lynn McNair to represent me in the divorce. You met her when you were here a few years ago. I was her attorney when she got her divorce and I respect her expertise."

"Does Nate know yet?"

"No! I want him to be surprised as hell when he's served divorce papers, like I was when I got Phil's report. Right now,

I have to make a list of all of our assets. I should have listened to you and gotten a prenup. I foolishly co-mingled most of my assets and now I'll probably have to share the majority of what I've worked so hard for with him. That makes me sick to my stomach, but it's my fault and I will have to live with it. I scheduled an appointment to meet with my accountant later this week so they can do a financial audit. Right now, I don't even care about the financial loss, I just want out of this marriage."

"Didn't you buy a house in Virginia recently?"

"Yes, we did; we closed in October. He persuaded me that it would be nice to have a weekend home away from the city. Can you believe that, purchasing a country home, while you already have a separate residence and family in North Carolina? I can't believe the nerve of him."

"What can I do?"

"Nothing but be my friend. It isn't like it's the first time I've gone through this. I changed my life insurance beneficiaries today. I'll be damned if something happens to me before our divorce is final and he gets another windfall. Recently he told me he was considering going into practice with a friend of his. What he didn't tell me was that he's trying to establish the firm in Charlotte. Since he doesn't have any money of his own, he was trying to get me to fund the venture. I guess he would have divorced me, or better yet, knowing him, continue doing things the way he's been doing them."

Jackie glanced at her watch, saw what time it was and said, "I apologize for ranting and raving, but I needed to blow off some steam. Anyway, I have to go, I have a meeting in less than an hour and I need to prepare for it. I'll call you later this evening."

# Chapter 38

Ashlee loved the east coast ever since she worked as a Congressional Aide there in 1996. She majored in architecture and planned to move there when she finished college. While she was in undergrad, she interned for two semesters at CJK Architects, a small firm in Washington. CJK specialized in physical land planning and architectural design of neighborhoods and communities. When she completed her undergraduate program, she immediately went to graduate school. When she finished she wanted to pursue being an architect at a large firm. Thanks to advice from her parents, she decided to pursue smaller firms where she would get a range of experience, and CJK Architects hired her.

She lived in a small one-bedroom apartment in Georgetown that was close to METRO, so she didn't need a car. When she wanted to get away, she would rent a car for the weekend, but there was so much to do in the city, that it was rare for her to leave. She had a good job, great friends and she dated occasionally, but nothing serious.

Sometimes she would think back to when she was young, when her mom was sick, and she knew she was very fortunate. Her mom wasn't sick anymore and she had a great supportive family. At twenty-eight, she was living the life.

Recently she had a nagging feeling that something wasn't quite right at home. In May, CJK Architects received notification that they were the recipients of the prestigious 2007 Architecture Firm Award. It is the highest honor the American Institute of Architects bestows on an architect firm. Her parents flew in to attend the ceremony and the impressive reception the firm held, then returned to Cincinnati the following day. It was unusual because they generally stayed with her for at least a week when they visited.

Lately when she called home in the evenings, her mom answered the phone. Her dad usually answered since he was always getting calls from people from the various programs he was involved with at night. She was used to him asking, "What's happening, baby girl?" when she called.

When she came home during the Fourth of July, her mom picked her up at the airport, which was again odd since her dad normally picked her up. They'd marvel at the Cincinnati skyline as they descended the hill in Kentucky, shortly before they crossed the Ohio River. He loved crossing the bridge into Ohio from Kentucky where the Greater Cincinnati Airport was located. He'd blow the car horn on the bridge and say it was his announcement of her return to Ohio.

Tonight she and her mom talked as they rode home, but her mom was much quieter than usual. When they reached home, her dad was asleep in his recliner in the family room. Ashlee gave him a kiss on the cheek.

"You've lost weight, Dad."

"That's because your mom went on strike, cooking less and less each day since you moved."

The next morning when she awoke, her parents were sitting at the kitchen table drinking coffee. She couldn't remember the last time her dad was home at 8:00 in the morning. As she started to make a comment, they told her that they needed to talk to her and asked her to join them at the table.

Then they told her, or rather, her dad told her that he was dying of cancer.

She sat there in shock, not believing what she was hearing. She began crying, "How long have you known, why didn't you call me, have you gotten a second opinion?" She went on and on, and when she looked up, she knew there were no options, even before her dad began speaking.

Then she went over to hug him, and she realized that he had lost more weight than she initially thought.

"We went to the best oncologist in Cincinnati and have gotten a second opinion. I have lung cancer and maybe only six months to live at most."

She spent a great deal of time with her dad that week. He explained that he accepted that he was dying and he was okay with it. He gave her a hug and told her that he knew she was hurting, but each of us is here for only a season. Then he said, "I'm happy I've had you and your mom in my life."

The night before she was due to return home, they sat on the porch. Ashlee told him she was going to ask her manager for a leave of absence, but he told her he didn't want her to alter her life in any way. He explained that she had done everything that he had ever wanted her to do but he didn't want her to watch him deteriorate.

When she arrived home, she immediately called her Aunt Jackie and told her everything, including the fact that her Dad didn't want her to take a leave of absence.

"I know, honey. It's hard on me too, but we have to abide by his wishes."

# Chapter 39

The house was deadly silent. The last few days, Bob slept most of the time. The hospice volunteers had told her to expect this as his time drew nearer. Now Dana spent most of her days checking on him and giving him his pain medications. The rest of the time, she was like a zombie. As she looked around her home, she could not remember the last time she cleaned the house. Friends had stopped by and spruced it up; but she didn't have the energy or desire to do anything.

It's amazing how things changed. For months, she would have done anything to have five minutes of rest and quiet. It seemed as if she was constantly up, either getting Bob's medications, assisting him in and out bed, or any of the other duties that come when you elect to care for a terminally ill patient at home. She never realized that the quiet she sought would signal that the end was close. She knew she was still in denial; all of those years, when she was in and out of hospitals, she always assumed she'd die first; she never thought she would lose him.

It was a bitter cold December day, with light snow covering their yard, but the sun was shining, so she opened the blinds in his room. Bob moved his head slightly, but didn't wake up. She thought, *it's probably because of the increased pain medication.* He looked so handsome with his shaved head. When the chemo began taking his hair out in clumps, he contacted his barber who came to the house and shaved his head bald. He told her he was trying to give her that Lou Gossett Jr. look which he kept after he discontinued chemo.

She walked through the house looking at the things they had accumulated. The study filled with plaques and commendations for his dedication to social issues, not only in his community, but also on a national level.

She thought, *what will happen to his projects, or his "babies" as he calls them, without him?* He felt that a leader should not determine the success of a venture. What mattered is whether the business can continue without the leader. *Will his projects flourish under new guidance?*

The family room with its African and Asian influences was where they spent countless hours talking, sharing a glass of wine, or watching videos. They did a lot of lovemaking in this room; cuddled up in front of the fireplace afterwards, talking and enjoying each other. Her mind wandered to the last time they made love and the tenderness. It was as if they were saying goodbye to that part of their life. Many people think that sex is the ultimate form of sharing, but your relationship goes to a new level when your spouse is dying. A hug, a kiss, an embrace, a smile, and the memories of all you have shared replace sex.

At 6:00 she heard a gentle knock on the door and it was Maurice, the evening hospice nurse. Hospice nurses had begun coming twice a day. After looking in and making the necessary adjustments, Maurice guided her gently into the living room. They sat down on the couch and he explained that Bob's time was nearing, maybe a day or two, but definitely not much more than that. His systems were shutting down and now would be a good time to notify anyone who wanted to say goodbye.

Dana knew this was coming: had known for months, but she still wasn't prepared. She felt her eyes well up, and tears began to run down her face. She couldn't believe she was crying. She thought she had cried herself out over the course of the last seven months. She excused herself, got up from the couch, went into the bathroom, got a tissue, and dried her eyes.

When she came back into the room, Maurice asked, "Would you like me to stay?"

"No, I'll be all right" she said, "I need a little time to myself before I make the necessary calls."

As Maurice departed, he gave her his personal cell phone number and told her to call him directly if she needed him adding, "I will be available anytime you need me."

She sat down trying to accept the fact that the end was nearing. She thought, *I am about to lose the man that has been my husband and my friend, and there is absolutely nothing I can do about it.* Tears continued to roll down her face. She decided to take this time to mourn. She knew that when she began to make the calls, she would have to be strong when her heart was breaking. It was difficult when he received the diagnosis that he had cancer, but nothing like this.

She finally got up and began making the calls that she knew she must make. Her first call was to Jackie. She was about to hang up when she realized that she had called her home number, instead of her office number, when Jackie answered. It was 6:00 p.m.; she couldn't believe she was home.

Even before Dana could say anything, Jackie asked, "Is it time?"

"Yes."

Dana and Jackie had talked about and planned what would need to be done, who to call. As she heard the catch in Jackie's voice, she knew that she was where she was; in a world of sheer disbelief. The planning was over, and now reality had set in, and with it, extreme pain.

Jackie told her that she and Ashlee would be in Cincinnati by midnight. They'd been packed for weeks and they had open tickets. That was exactly what Bob would want.

From the moment she made the call to Jackie, time flew by. She made the other necessary calls, her parents, Bob's cousins and a few close friends. Jackie and Ashlee arrived, and Dana thought she saw him open his eyes for a second when Ashlee came in the room, but she wasn't sure. Throughout the night and early morning, they took turns sitting by his bedside.

The next morning, Jackie and Ashlee were in the kitchen drinking coffee. Dana joined them for a moment and suggested that Ashlee try to get a little sleep, so she went to her old bedroom to lie down.

Last month, they had moved Bob's hospital bed into the family room. Dana returned to the room and began adjusting the blind, when she heard what she knew was his last breath. She didn't know how she knew, but she did. When she turned around, he was lying on the bed and he looked at peace. The pain that ravaged his body for the last few months was finally over. She sat next to him for a while, held his hand and told him how much she loved him. Then, she got up and called to Jackie, who was still in the kitchen sipping coffee. Jackie stayed with Bob's body while she went upstairs to tell Ashlee.

Ashlee was devastated, "How could this happen so fast? I was just in the room with Dad."

She and Ashlee came back downstairs and sat beside him with tears flowing down their faces. Jackie stood by the window, softly crying and hugging herself.

After a few minutes, Dana left the room and began making the stream of calls that she needed to make. Hospice came immediately and prepared the body and a few close friends and family came to say goodbye before the mortuary arrived to take the body.

She wondered *how a living, vibrant human being could be reduced to "the body" in such a short period of time.*

Dana and Bob had discussed the final arrangements, and although it was painful at the time, she was grateful now. She remembered what they had gone through when Bob's oldest aunt died unexpectedly. Relatives were caught up in their emotions and many hurtful words were spoken. The day after his aunt's funeral Bob scheduled an appointment with their attorney and had him update their wills. When he received the diagnosis of lung cancer, he contacted their minister, and they sat down together and made his final arrangements.

Now Dana was riding in a limousine following behind the hearse taking her husband of 23 years to his resting spot. The ceremony at the church had been beautiful. The seniors from the community group he worked with handled all the music. He would have been so proud of them. Many of them made remarks. She vaguely remembered Miss Johnson saying how much she would miss her "boyfriend"; her nickname for Bob when she first met him, and she smiled. She sat through the gravesite service with Jackie and Ashlee by her side, and her parents and brothers close by, as they listened to the military's 21-gun salute.

Later she stood in the reception line at the church hall and thanked people for coming. Bob didn't like reception lines. She remembered him joking with her about it when they were making his final arrangements, saying, "I'm glad I won't have to endure another one of those."

Finally, at 10:00 that night, Jackie told those who were still at the house that Dana and Ashlee had been up since early that morning and needed to get some rest. When everyone was gone, Dana thanked Jackie for being so diplomatic and they both had a good laugh. They both knew that there were times when Jackie and diplomacy were an oxymoron.

Ashlee came downstairs and gave them a look like how could they be laughing. When they told her what they were laughing about, she started laughing too. She had heard enough stories about her aunt and she had even been in court with her once. She knew that she could be fierce under the wrong circumstances. Then they hugged each other, and between laughter and tears, they agreed that this is what Bob would want.

# Chapter 40

The days following the funeral were miserable for everyone. The funeral was held on Friday morning so friends and relatives had all left by Sunday afternoon, except Jackie. People continued stopping by to express their condolences, but it was awkward and painful. In the evenings, they sat around the fireplace talking. Ashlee said she couldn't believe everything was over; the last week still seemed unreal to her. A neighbor, Mrs. Singleton, told her that things would get back to normal soon, but she said that for her things would never get back to normal because for her, normal was having her dad.

As she talked, Dana went over, sat beside her, and said, "I know you're hurting, we all are. Mrs. Singleton was trying to help. Unfortunately, people don't realize that sometimes it's better to say nothing."

Ashlee continued, "Each morning I wake up thinking this is a bad dream, but then I go down to the kitchen and there is no evidence that Dad has been up. When I came home, he always left my favorite coffee mug on the counter. Now I'm the one starting the coffeemaker in the morning. I find myself scooping out coffee with tears rolling down my face."

They tried to keep busy, but Bob had handled most things, so they had very little to do. Ashlee began writing thank you notes; leaving a few for her Mom to personally write. Each day Ashlee drove her dad's car to the cemetery, even though the weather was bitterly cold, and sat in his car crying and looking at his gravesite.

They agreed that they didn't want to be in Cincinnati for Christmas. There were way too many memories. They discussed going back east, but Jackie said she really didn't want to deal with the airports during the holidays. Dana's parents were going to Atlanta to be with her brothers. Eventually they decided that they would drive to Virginia and spend Christmas with Gran. Aunt Mildred left for Virginia following the funeral, but she would be leaving on a cruise the day after Christmas. Dana and Ashlee had visited Gran numerous times, but never during Christmas.

Dana said, "I'll make our hotel arrangements."

Jackie quickly said, "No, we can all stay at Gran's, it might be a little tight, but she'd be offended if you stayed in a hotel."

They enjoyed the time they spent with Gran. Although she was in her nineties and had lost weight over the years, she was such a joy. She and Aunt Mildred cooked every food imaginable and they sat around the house talking, eating and enjoying each other's company on Christmas Day.

Aunt Mildred left the following morning for her cruise, and while they were at the airport, they arranged for Ashlee to return home later in the week. Some friends of hers were having a New Year's Eve party, and she was looking forward to attending.

While they were at the airport, Dana said, "Jackie, if you want to change your flight and leave from here that will be okay. I can drive back to Ohio by myself. I know you will be going back to work right after New Year's and you probably need to get some rest. You worked so hard to ensure that the services went smoothly. You've got to be tired, both mentally and physically."

"No, I don't have to be at work; I took a leave of absence."

"You didn't tell me that."

"I know I wanted to wait. Why don't we talk about it on our drive back to Cincinnati?"

Jackie and Dana said goodbye to Gran and left early on December 31st for their trip back to Ohio to avoid New Year's Eve traffic. Aunt Mildred had returned the day before. She offered to fix breakfast for them before they left, but they said they weren't hungry and would stop for breakfast later.

They had been on the road for about three hours, talking and listening to oldie CD's, when they decided to stop for breakfast at a pancake house. After they placed their orders, Jackie said, "I guess it's time I explain why I took a leave of absence from the firm. There have been a lot of things happening in my life and the last three months have been such a blur for me that I don't really know where to begin."

"Do you remember the day I called you and you were at the coffee shop?"

"Sure, that was one of the few times I was away from Bob."

"You asked me about a story you were reading in the Cincinnati Enquirer that involved a plane crash in the DC area and I changed the subject."

"Yes, but what does that have to do with you taking a leave of absence?"

Jackie took a deep breath before continuing, "When you brought up the subject, I wasn't ready to talk to you yet." She shook her head before she continued, "Dana, Nate died in that plane crash."

"What," asked Dana incredulously? "Jackie, why didn't you tell me?"

"Dana, I called you the morning after it happened, but that was the morning Bob had to be rushed to the hospital. The ambulance was on the way and you were frantic. I could even hear sirens in the background. I thought about calling you later, but I decided not to. I had already burdened you for years with my problems with Nate. I couldn't do it, not with Bob being so sick; besides there was absolutely nothing that could be done. I felt that you had too much on your plate. It wasn't like Nate and I were together, we'd been estranged for almost two years."

"Ironically, the night he died, he was in town earlier in the day so we could finalize our divorce. I thought that it was finally going to be over, but when Lynn told him I would get the condo in Vail, he went ballistic. He began cursing, even calling me a bitch and stormed out of the office. Later that night airline personnel notified me that Nate was a passenger on the flight from Dulles Airport to Charlotte that crashed shortly after takeoff."

"Sometimes it's hard for me to believe that Nate is dead, but I have several copies of his death certificate in my desk drawer to know that it's true."

"I still can't believe you didn't tell me. You didn't have to go through this by yourself. How did you handle going to the funeral?"

Jackie responded, "First of all, I didn't go through it all by myself, Aunt Mildred was there for me. As for the funeral, I chose not to attend. It would have been such a farce, he had his new family. I didn't think his parents would appreciate me being there."

Before Dana could say anything, Jackie continued. "Anyway, since we weren't divorced, I was the next of kin so I asked Lynn McNair to act as my Power of Attorney. As my divorce attorney, she was definitely familiar with Nate. She handled everything, from contacting Nate's parents so they could make the final arrangements, to coordinating the funeral arrangements and transferring payment to the mortuary in Charlotte. I went to the morgue the day before the body was released and said my farewell."

Jackie sighed, "My insurance company contacted me weeks later and notified me that Nate hadn't changed the beneficiary on his life insurance policies and that there was a double indemnity clause in the event of an accident. During our marriage we agreed to carry high insurance coverage because the rates were nominal and we wanted to make sure each of us would be in a good financial position in the event anything should happen."

They had been sitting in the restaurant for thirty minutes; the waitress brought their food and checked with them when she saw that neither of them was eating. They assured her that there was nothing wrong with the food, they weren't really hungry, but asked her to replenish their coffee.

"I was surprised when you mentioned the story. I knew you hadn't been reading the paper or watching the news, so you can't imagine how shocked I was when you found out, but I still couldn't say anything. Anyway, last week the surviving relatives were notified that the airline was at fault since a critical aircraft part was defective. The plane was long overdue for a scheduled maintenance overhaul, and the defective part would have been identified if the company had performed the maintenance work."

"Wow, it could have been avoided. Does Ashlee know about this?"

"Yes, I had to tell her because they listed the victims' names in the local papers and I knew she would see it. I made her promise not to tell you, so don't be upset with her."

"I'm not going to be upset with her, you asked her to keep a confidence and she did, but I am concerned about you. What do you plan to do?"

"I'm not sure; I'm on an extended leave of absence from the firm. I need to try to find me again. The irony is that I have always wanted to be wealthy. Well, I got my wish, between not having to share any of my assets since the divorce was not finalized, the insurance proceeds and the projected proceeds from the lawsuit against Southeast Com Regional Airlines. I have more money than I will ever spend. Unfortunately, the cost has been too high. Gran always told me that money by itself will never bring you happiness, and she is definitely right."

They asked the server for the check and some fruit to take with them since neither one of them had touched their breakfast. Soon they were back on the road.

# Chapter 41

Jackie and Dana didn't talk very much as they continued driving; both of them deep in their own thoughts. As they crossed the Ohio state line, Dana finally spoke, "I've been thinking why don't you stay at the house with me for a while? You know Bob always said the fourth bedroom was for you."

Before Jackie could respond, she said, "This is so ironic. Our first marriages ended around the same time and now we have lost our second husbands within months of each other. I think staying together might be good for both of us. Maybe we can help each other during this healing period. You don't have to give me an answer right now, but I would like you to think about it."

"Aren't you going to be returning to work soon?"

"I don't think so; I have an opportunity to take an early retirement. The county is downsizing and they asked for volunteers and I'm thinking of doing it. Bob's death, and now hearing about Nate's, makes me think that maybe I need to enjoy as much of life as possible. Do the things I really want to do. Right now, I want to take some time and think. We have insurance on the house in the event of one of our deaths, so the house will be paid off and we don't have any debt. With Bob's pension, the insurance proceeds, and my retirement, I think I'll be okay."

"You'll be more than okay; I have a substantial sum of money that I plan to give you as soon as everything is finalized."

"You don't have to do that, I really don't need any money."

"No, this is something I definitely want to do; it's only good to have this kind of money if you can share it with someone. I've made arrangements for Gran and Aunt Mildred, and I definitely want my best friend to share in this windfall."

"We can discuss that later."

When Dana and Jackie arrived at the house, they promptly ordered Chinese food, made a pitcher of Mimosa's and watched a couple of movies. They stayed up late reminiscing about their friendship and talking about their dreams, ones fulfilled and ones yet to be fulfilled.

"I can't believe that we're 54 and have been friends for over 35 years. Girl, we have gone through so much together." Jackie laughed, and said, "I am so glad that walls can't talk."

"We have had some interesting times, especially when we were in Oakland. You know I never went back. I didn't want to take a chance of running into Cameron. I wonder how everything worked out for him and his wife."

"After you left, I ran into him occasionally at a local coffee shop and I remember thinking how sad he looked. Later we were members of the same bar association and saw each other at meetings, but that's been years ago."

"It's so weird, but last month I thought about him, and he stayed on my mind. I hadn't thought about him in years. I hope that wherever he is, he's okay."

They both agreed that they had not envisioned their lives turning out the way they had. Dana remarked, "Life got in the way, we were young, and we didn't realize that there would be so many things that would be out of our control."

"I thought that if I worked extremely hard, I would make up for all the years Gran raised me and we didn't have very much. I'd be able to give her anything she wanted, but all she ever wanted was for me to be happy. I focused so much on my career and the financial aspects of my life that now I have money, and that's pretty much all I have. I should have realized that although we didn't have much money when I was growing up, we did have genuine love. Now I have to make my life right; get off the materialistic track. That's my goal for 2008."

"I'm like you, I need to refocus. I really haven't done anywhere near the traveling I planned to do. Bob and I traveled but nothing like I wanted; with my passport filled to capacity."

Jackie laughed, and said, "I loved my play brother, but traveling was not on the top of his list of things to do." She continued, "All jokes aside, Dana, if you want to travel, let me know where you want to go. I can pay your expenses to travel around the world, if that's what you want to do. I read about a one year trip around the world where you stay at some impressive hotels and they have exceptional tours in each country you visit."

"Thanks, but that's not exactly what I have in mind. Last year I read an article about international opportunities to volunteer and see other countries. It was something that I thought I would like to explore. I knew Bob wouldn't be interested, but I kept the article. I think it would be nice to travel, see the world and volunteer at the same time. After I get everything settled, I'm going to look into it."

Right before midnight, they decided to have a prayer session. They turned off the lights in the house and lit candles. They thanked God for all the blessings they had that year and for the people who were brought into their lives, and for those who were no longer with them. Then they each blew out a candle in remembrance of Bob and Nate.

They both cried and Jackie acknowledged that it was the first time she cried for Nate since she received notification of his death. Then she added, "I needed to do this. I was so mad at him, for what he said at our last meeting, for having another family, and for not changing his life insurance. I think I was even mad about not being able to attend his funeral service, although that was my decision. I know it's not rational, but it is how I felt."

Ashlee called at midnight to wish them Happy New Year. Finally, they acknowledged that they were exhausted.

Before they headed to bed, Jackie asked, "Is that offer to stay here still good?"

"Most definitely."

Jackie smiled, "Then I guess we'll be roommates again."

2008

# Chapter 42

Overall, Dana did as well as she could. Sometimes she would hear a song or think of something that Bob might say and she would become sad, but each day she got a little stronger. One of the hardest things for Dana was getting rid of Bob's clothes. It was an unseasonably cold winter, so she dry cleaned his coats and donated them to a men's homeless shelter. His clothes were different; she found it hard to part with them. Each time she went into his closet she could smell his scent; the cologne that he had worn for years lingered in the air. She decided not to force the issue. She knew that at some point she would know when and how to dispose of his clothes, but not now.

Jackie finalized Bob's estate and Dana was surprised to learn that in addition to the life insurance policy she was aware of, Bob had an additional policy in the amount of $250,000, payable to her. When she found out, she wasn't surprised. It was like Bob, always wanting to ensure her security. She met with a financial adviser, who helped her determine her long-term financial needs and establish a balanced growth and income portfolio. When she was comfortable knowing that she would be in a good financial position, she decided that she no longer had any interest in returning to work, so she submitted her paperwork for early retirement.

"I feel like I am back in college and planning my future again," she told Jackie. "As I look back, I realize that life got in the way most of the time after I left Wilberforce. Either it was Michael on drugs, becoming a single parent, or my years struggling with the brain tumor, and now Bob dying. I'm not going to let that happen now. I've been given a clean canvas and I can do anything I want. Now I can fulfill my dream to travel and see the world. Ashlee is grown, I'm in good health and I don't have to worry about a job anymore. Retirement is definitely liberating. Right now, it's all about me and I plan to take this time and enjoy it."

She explored various international volunteer opportunities for seniors and went through a wealth of information; highlighting areas of special interest to her. Ultimately, she decided to apply to International Senior Citizens Ambassadors Organization (ISCAO) because they had the most flexible program, allowing her to volunteer for up to a year without returning to the states, if she chose to. In addition, there was sufficient flexibility in their schedules and vacation periods for volunteers to see other countries.

She knew she would like to volunteer in Africa, but she wasn't exactly sure which region until she researched the continent. She decided on Ghana because of the country's history. She planned to visit many sights including The Du Bois Centre in Accra, and the Elmina Castles along with Fort St. Jago, all designated as World Heritage Sites.

She planned to tour as much of Africa as she could while she was there, including Senegal and the Ivory Coast, which were

French-speaking countries. She hired a teacher who taught French at the local high school to tutor her so she could be conversant in the language. She wasn't sure exactly when she would apply for the program, but she wanted to make sure that she was prepared when she did.

In June, she applied to the organization and was surprised when she received acceptance for the January 2009 session. Initially, she would train in New Orleans and then go on to Ghana where she would volunteer as a social worker in a hospital. She was excited; this was her first step toward fulfilling her dream to see the world.

Jackie was happy for Dana for following her dream, but she was struggling with what to do with her life. She knew she needed to make some major changes. She considered going to a counselor or psychologist, but decided that she couldn't expect help until she was honest with herself. She had achieved all the goals she once felt were important - wealth, partnership in a prestigious law firm and owner of numerous rental properties. She didn't need a shrink to tell her why she was so unhappy. She didn't have the medical term, but she knew it had to do with her obsession with success. She suspected it was her way of distancing herself from her childhood poverty and her way to show and reaffirm her achievements. Now there weren't any more financial or career goals she wanted to attain.

She knew that her biggest challenge would be to change her focus, not be as goal oriented. She thought that maybe it was time to leave her position at the firm. As hard as she had worked to make partner, she no longer had the zest for practicing law she once had. Now she wanted to take time to explore her interests. She thought that this would be a good time for her to start giving back and that would require a commitment from her of more than a check. She acknowledged that she had worked hard and many people had faith in her and helped her throughout the years. Now it was her turn to reciprocate, not necessarily to those who helped her, but to others in need.

She decided that she would like to explore nonprofit work and see where that would take her. With her years of experience, she had formed numerous charitable trusts. She needed to find a cause that she felt passionate about since she knew she would be excellent at establishing a nonprofit.

She considered working with teens, especially college students, looking for a career in the field of law. She contacted Columbia and resumed working with their recruitment office. She did presentations for them at two schools in Cincinnati and one at her old high school in Virginia. Although she enjoyed it and felt it was a noble cause, she quickly discovered that working with teens wasn't what she wanted to do on a full-time basis.

After she attended a senior citizen's board meeting with Dana, she began to wonder if there was a need in her hometown for a new senior citizen's facility. She knew that they had a facility in her hometown. Miss Emma who was Gran's roommate until she got Alzheimer's, had lived in one and was unhappy there. She began to think about building a senior facility in her hometown similar to the one Bob had begun in Ohio. When she told Gran what she was considering, she was happy. She said it would be a good idea, since the current seniors' building was old and run down.

She traveled to Charlottesville, spending time with Gran, and trying to garner community interest in what she determined to be a much-needed new senior facility. Unfortunately, she was unable to raise sufficient interest or funding.

When Dana decided that she would go to Africa, Jackie chose to stay in Cincinnati and volunteer at the senior citizens facility that Bob had started. Ted Farmington was the director now. He was in his early sixties, spry and had the same passion and drive for working with seniors that Bob had. He was exploring the feasibility of opening another facility in the city and could use someone to assist him. It would give her the chance to learn the operation from the ground up and gain the experience she would need to start a new facility in her hometown, if she chose to pursue that avenue again.

Jackie returned to Washington monthly, for the first few months after she decided to stay with Dana, but gradually her visits became more and more infrequent. On her last visit, she walked through her condominium and realized there were only a few things that she really treasured. When Ashlee mentioned that her lease would be up soon, she asked her if she would be interested in moving into her place.

"I would definitely like to, but I don't make that kind of money."

"You can afford it. It's paid for so you would only have to pay the Homeowner's Association fees and utilities. I haven't moved my furniture, so you can have it, or I'll donate it."

"Are you sure?"

"I'm definitely sure."

Jackie began working with Ted on a daily basis and had to acknowledge that the pace was very slow. She definitely did not miss the long hours she worked at the firm, but she was beginning to miss working at the law firm. Working as an attorney had been her primary dream and focus for nearly forty years.

One evening during dinner, Jackie told Dana, "I like what I'm doing with Ted, but I have to admit, I'm getting a little bored."

"I've been watching you and wondering when you'd come to that conclusion."

"Why didn't you say anything?"

"Because I knew you needed to work things out for yourself. I also know that from the time I first met you, you have been in love with every aspect of practicing law. I remember when we first met and your eyes lit up when you told me you wanted to be an attorney. That hasn't really changed over the years."

"I agree I do love being an attorney. I wish there were some way for me to mesh my passion for law with my desire to work in the nonprofit sector."

"I have confidence in you, you'll find an answer."

# Chapter 43

Today was the one year anniversary of Bob's death. Dana lay in bed that morning, holding a pillow to her chest and softly crying; she missed him so much. Each day she went through her daily routine, her new norm as she called it, but there was always this ache and today the pain was excruciating.

Finally she forced herself to get out of bed. As she was leaving her bedroom she glanced over at Bob's closet, which she hadn't opened in months. Right then she decided that today would be the day she donated his clothes. One year was enough time and she knew that he would want others to have them. She returned to the room and selected a few items that she wanted to keep, a pair of cufflinks, a pair of pajamas, and a white shirt with his initials on the cuffs. Then she called two of his close friends to see if there was anything they would like as a keepsake. She also contacted Ashlee and then began folding the remaining items. She smiled, realizing this was exactly what Bob would want her to do on the anniversary of his death; do something that would help others. Hours later, when she was finished packing all his clothes, she felt a sense of peace.

She went to the kitchen and made a fresh pot of coffee. She sat at the table thinking about Bob and she knew that her decision to leave the country and volunteer in Africa was exactly what she needed to do. Being in the house every day with all the memories, was too hard.

She had approximately one month before her departure and she was ready. She was surprised that the entire process had gone relatively smooth. There had been a delay in processing one of her visas, but it finally arrived last week. She had also taken all the recommended immunizations. The location of the two-week training session changed to Fort Lauderdale, Florida, since a large number of the trainees would be volunteering in Africa. Volunteers paid their own airfare, so being closer to their ultimate destination would reduce the cost.

That evening Dana and Jackie had a long discussion. Jackie said, "You were right, as usual, about my figuring out what I needed to do. I am setting up a trust fund for Nate's children. I was angry with him, but when I finally forgave him for all the pain he caused me, I still didn't feel right."

"Gran and I talked and she told me that the reason I was still feeling bad was that I hadn't done the right thing by his children." She said, 'You had every right to be mad at Nate, but his children had nothing to do with it. You need to make sure they're taken care of.' She was right; they had nothing to do with my problems with Nate. The trust will fund their education."

"It's amazing, as soon as I decided to establish the trust fund for Nate's children, things started to fall in place. I told Franklin I was thinking about leaving the firm and he asked me to consider heading up the company that we are acquiring in Cincinnati. We had talked about branching out of the area, but none of the partners wanted to relocate to the Midwest. It's a great opportunity for the firm, and it's perfect for me. I'll be back in the main office once a month, but I will spend the rest of the time establishing the new office."

"That sounds like a great plan."

2009

# Chapter 44

The day she was scheduled to leave, Dana went to the cemetery and spent time at Bob's gravesite. It was bitterly cold and she stood shivering in her heavy winter coat, speaking softly, "I'm going to be away awhile, but you will always be with me no matter how far the distance."

On the way to the airport, Jackie asked Dana if she was excited.

"I have mixed emotions. On one hand, I am very excited, but I'm also a little apprehensive. Saying you want to live outside of the United States and actually doing it are two different things, especially at my age. One thing is that from the time I decided to apply, I have not had any second thoughts. Things will work out fine."

Jackie helped her get her bags out of the car when they arrived at the airport.

Dana said, "I love you, girlfriend, and thank you for being with me this last year," and quickly hugged her.

"No, thank you for allowing me to stay; now go on inside before we both have a meltdown. I'll talk to you later tonight."

The flight was smooth and in no time, Dana was in Florida, and it was a beautiful, warm, sunny day. She thought, *I can see why people head here for the winter.* As soon as she located her bags, she headed for the shuttle bus that took her to the conference center where the volunteers would be staying and training conducted. She was surprised at the number of people who were registering; she hadn't thought there would be so many. She could hear people around her discussing areas where they would be volunteering. Some were going to South America and others to China, but there was a large contingency going to various parts of Africa.

When she settled in her room, she took time to look at the first week's itinerary. They would receive an overview of the program and overall expectations as well as participate in various team-building exercises. The second week they would break into their individual groups and address specifics about the country where they would volunteer.

The first days were great and Dana made friends easily. Everyone was as excited as she was, but also a little apprehensive. The group bonded quickly, and Dana and a woman named Judith Sexton found out that they shared common interests. They both wanted to travel, but had not done so because of family commitments. Both had lost their spouses, now they were making a dream a reality. Others were volunteering because they were retired and wanted to give back to others less fortunate. Regardless of why they were there, they all agreed that they felt it was a good decision.

At the end of the week, they had a small closing ceremony and the volunteers were informed which group they would be working with the following week. Neither Dana nor Judith had been to Ft. Lauderdale before, so they spent the weekend exploring the city.

On Monday morning, Dana got up early and worked out before her training session began. As she was returning to her room, she noticed a tall, slender man getting a newspaper in the lobby. She wondered if he was one of the instructors who would be conducting training this week since she hadn't seen him the previous week. He was a distance from her so she couldn't see his face.

When she arrived at the auditorium, she sat in the front row. In the distance, she could see John Kingman, the program coordinator, talking with a group of instructors on the stage. She was reviewing her package as John welcomed everyone and started the session.

"Welcome to the 2009 International Senior Citizens Ambassadors Organization training session for volunteers. This week you will be working with current volunteers who have taken the same journey you will take next week. They will be working with you for the first two days as a group, and then you'll break into smaller groups for the area you're assigned to work. At the end of the week, you will be more than able to handle your assignment. So without further ado, let me introduce our illustrious faculty team. First, Amy Rusterling from Memphis, Tennessee, will be the lead instructor." As Dana looked up, he said, "Next, Cameron Mitchell from Decatur, Alabama." The program coordinator introduced the other two instructors, but Dana didn't hear anything else he said.

Instead, she stared. Yes, it was the man she had seen earlier buying a paper. It was Cameron, a little leaner, now with gray hair and a beard, but it was definitely Cameron Mitchell.

Amy said, "We usually start by telling about our experiences in Africa, but today I'd like to switch things around a little, so why don't each of you introduce yourselves and say a little about why you're here."

Cameron glanced up as the first two people gave their information and looked back down to take notes. She was next, and before he looked up, she said, "My name is Dana Adams Richardson."

She was looking directly at him, so she saw the shock on his face when he heard her voice, one that he had not heard in over twenty-five years.

When the last volunteer finished, Amy said, "Let's take a two-minute stretch break."

Cameron immediately came down from the stage and approached Dana, giving her a big hug.

"I can't believe this. I saw the roster and saw that there was a woman named Dana A. Richardson from Cincinnati, but I didn't make the connection."

"I was also shocked when John introduced you. How have you been?"

"Times up," Amy said. Cameron paused before heading to the stage and said, "We have so much to catch up on. Do you have plans for lunch?"

"No, not really."

"There's a great Cuban restaurant close by. Will you join me?"

"Sure!"

When the break ended, the instructors gave their bios. Dana knew a lot of Cameron's early information, but she was surprised that he retired in 2007 and moved back to his hometown. When the instructors completed their bios, they did an overview of what the volunteers could expect during the week and opened the session for questions and answers.

Amy suggested that they take an early lunch break and before they left, Cameron officially introduced Dana to his fellow instructor. He explained that they were good friends when he lived in the Bay Area, but had lost contact with each other over the years.

As they left, Amy said, "I'm sure you have a lot of catching up to do."

Cameron laughed, and said, "You're right, something like 25 years of catch up."

They walked slowly to the restaurant. He said, "I am still shocked, where do we start?"

"I'm like you; I'm still in shock, too."

He said, "Well, tell me what you've been doing. How's your daughter, Ashlee, doing?"

"She's an architect and lives in DC."

"I can't believe it, she was only four or five when I last saw her."

"She was three when we left the Bay Area, and she will be 31 this year."

"No way!"

"It's hard for me to believe sometimes, too. She is doing great. I am really proud of her."

"What is your friend Jackie doing these days?"

"She's a partner in a large law practice which is expanding their offices to the Midwest. As of next week she'll be starting up their Cincinnati office."

Cameron smiled. "From what I remember about her, I am definitely not surprised."

By that time, they had reached the restaurant and ordered their food.

"I heard that you married when you went back to Ohio."

"Yes, I did, but my husband died in 2007."

"Wow, I'm sorry to hear that."

"Thanks, I appreciate that. He was a great guy and a good husband; sometimes it's hard to believe he's gone."

"What about you, you live in Alabama now?"

"Yes, right after Eileen and I divorced, I retired and joined ISCAO, and my first assignment was in Alabama. I spent three months there and it felt good being back at home after being away so many years, but I really wanted to see the world. When I got an opportunity, I applied to work in Africa and spent six months there, mostly in Ghana and South Africa. I returned to the States when my dad was dying. Although our parents are gone, neither my brother nor I want to sell the house, so now when I'm in the States I live in the house that I grew up in. It's worked out well since I always have a place to stay when I return to the States."

When they finished lunch, they had just enough time to get back to the training session. On the way back Cameron said, "I'd like to talk with you more, if that's okay with you."

"Definitely, I'd like that too."

"I know Amy has plans for our team to have a group dinner tonight, but how about dinner tomorrow night?"

"Sure."

As soon as the session was over, Dana went to her room and called Jackie.

"You're not going to believe what happened. Cameron is one of my instructors."

"Cameron Mitchell?"

"Yes." She told her about them having lunch and that he asked about her and Ashlee.

"How does he look?"

"He looks great, he's aged, but who hasn't? He's taken good care of himself."

"What happened to his wife?"

"He told me he's divorced, but he didn't go into any details."

"That's interesting."

"I can't believe this. I never expected to see him again. Remember I told you that when Bob was ill and I spent a lot of time by myself, I found myself wondering how he was doing. This is so weird, someone I have not seen in over twenty-five years and now I will be working with him."

"What's next?"

"We're going to have dinner tomorrow evening."

"Are you okay?"

"Sure, but I have to admit this feels a little unreal. All afternoon it was hard for me to concentrate on what the instructors were saying. A couple of times when I looked up, Cameron was looking at me."

"He's probably still as shocked as you are."

"You're not going to believe what happened to me today. I was at the office working with Ted on some issues for the new senior citizens complex and he asked me to have lunch with him tomorrow."

"I'm surprised he took so long. He's been looking at you since you got there."

"It's probably a business issue."

"Trust me; it's more than a business issue."

The next morning, Dana took more care with her makeup than she had in a while. She had to admit that she was flattered when she saw Cameron watching her; it felt good.

That evening, they met for an early dinner at a French restaurant that overlooked the water and talked about what they had been doing for the last twenty- five plus years.

Dana told him about Bob, the brain tumor, her work and her family. She explained why she decided to take an early retirement and join ISCAO. She was amazed at how easy it was for her to talk to him. It was as if they picked up where they had left off many years ago.

Over drinks, Cameron said, "After you left, I was miserable, but I was determined to make my marriage work. There was no way I could leave Eileen knowing that she had MS. Laney grew by leaps and bounds and I got a lot of personal satisfaction from my work."

"After the first few years, Eileen became closed-mouthed about her condition so I quit going to the doctor with her. I relied on her to keep me up to date on how she was doing. Periodically, she would tell me she was having a bout with MS, but nothing too serious. She would take a few days off from work and then seem to be okay."

"About five years ago, the college was trying to get support from the medical community and find a way for some of our promising students to pursue medical school. We had a number of noted physicians from various areas speak at a symposium and one of them was Eileen's physician, Dr. Berg."

"I hadn't seen him in years, so after the session was over, I went over and introduced myself. He remembered me and I thanked him for the great care he gave Eileen."

"He said, 'Well, I'm happy everything turned out okay for her. The unfortunate thing about MS is that it can easily be misdiagnosed, which happened in her case.' I was getting ready to tell him he must have me confused with another patient's spouse, but someone interrupted us."

"Later that night, I mentioned the conversation to Eileen and she told me that she had changed physicians years ago and quickly changed the subject. I would have dropped the issue, but a few months later the college held a reception for members of the business community and Dr. Berg attended. He approached me and asked how Eileen was doing and I said she was doing fine."

"Then he said, 'It's been over twenty years since I last saw her. I'm glad to know that she's doing well. Unfortunately the symptoms she had mirrored MS, but thanks to improvements in the medical field, we finally got her an accurate diagnosis.'"

"I didn't mention anything about the discussion to Eileen. The next week, I requested that our medical insurance company provide me with a detailed record of our medical records for the last fifteen years. When I received them, I reviewed them and there were no charges for neurological services. As a matter of a fact, other than annual routine exams, Eileen rarely went to any doctor."

"I was puzzled, based on what Dr. Berg said and the medical records, Eileen was lying, but I wasn't sure why. When she arrived home that evening, I told her about the reception and my talk with Dr. Berg. Then I told her I had a copy of our medical records and there were no charges for any neurological services in recent years. I took the envelope out of my briefcase and gave it to her."

"When she realized that there was no way out of telling the truth, she told me what she'd done. As Dr. Berg told me, after a few years she wasn't mirroring the symptoms they expected. They had her take a battery of new tests that were on the market. That's when they found out that she didn't have MS."

"I asked her, 'Why didn't you tell me?'"

"She said, 'At first, when we separated, I did want a divorce. You weren't going in the right direction, but I got scared when I was diagnosed with MS. I knew that you had only stayed because I was ill. I suspected that you were seriously involved with someone during the separation. When I found out that I didn't have MS, I was afraid that you might leave so I decided not to tell you.'"

"I was floored when she told me. All these years she had been living a lie. At first, I tried to make it work, but then I got angry. I thought about how I had given up part of my life because I felt it was wrong to leave my spouse when she was ill. I remember there were times when I wanted to leave and I would recall my marriage vows. I started advancing at Laney and receiving recognition for leading one of the most innovative and fast growing colleges in the country. I became Dean of the Business and Mathematics School, which fit into Eileen's view of an acceptable position for me. She did everything she could to maintain our image. Shortly after I discovered she had been lying about having MS all those years, I filed for divorce. When it was close to e time for the divorce to be finalized, I submitted my retirement papers."

Dana sat there quietly, sipping a glass of wine while he talked. All she could say was, "I am so sorry."

He said, "I'm okay now. It's over. I had put many of my dreams on the back burner. When I found out about this opportunity to volunteer around the world, I knew it was exactly what I wanted and needed to do. Seeing you again tells me that there are definitely some benefits I never would have expected."

They spent the next few evenings going to dinner with other volunteers, but they always found time to spend a couple of hours talking at the end of the night.

On the last evening, they walked barefoot on the beach after the team dinner.

"Tomorrow is going to be busy with everyone preparing to leave and we probably won't have much time to talk," Cameron said. "I know that we plan to stay in contact via Skype and e-mail, but I need to tell you something tonight. The last few days have been the happiest I have had since you left Oakland. I am so glad that we have been able to connect again. Since we reconnected, I have been trying to figure out what to do. I realize that I let life get in the way once and I lost you. I am not going to make that mistake again. Yesterday, I requested a transfer to your team and they approved the request. I will be joining you in two weeks, as soon as they get a replacement for me here."

Dana looked in his eyes, and said, "I can't believe this is happening. Less than a month ago, there was no way I would have thought I'd ever be happy again. The last few days have been unbelievable. When we talk, it's like we've always been together; that there was never a separation."

There was a gentle breeze and Dana shivered. Cameron pulled her gently to him and wrapped his arms around her. She looked up and they kissed for the first time in over twenty-five years before they walked to her room.

## THE END

16991145R00194

Made in the USA
Charleston, SC
21 January 2013